# A PARALLEL LIFE AND OTHER STORIES

# A PARALLEL LIFE AND OTHER STORIES

BY

ROBIN BEEMAN

CHRONICLE BOOKS • SAN FRANCISCO

Some of the stories in this collection have previously appeared
in the following magazines:

"Taking Fire" in *Ascent;* "Three Rivers" in *Apalachee Quarterly;*
"Life Signs," "UFO," and "Bougainvillea" in *Fiction Network.*

Copyright © 1992 by Robin Beeman. All rights reserved.
No part of this book may be reproduced in any form without
written permission from the publisher.

Printed in the United States of America.

Library of Congress Cataloging in Publication Data:

Beeman, Robin.
A parallel life and other stories / by Robin Beeman.
p.     cm.
ISBN 0-8118-0085-7
I. Title.
PS3552.E346P37    1992          91-31069
813'.54—dc20              CIP

Cover design: Sharon Smith
Interior design and composition: Ann Flanagan Typography
Cover art: Dan May

Distributed in Canada by Raincoast Books,
112 East Third Avenue, Vancouver, B.C. V5T 1C8

10   9   8   7   6   5   4   3   2   1

Chronicle Books
275 Fifth Street
San Francisco, CA 94103

# Contents

# A PARALLEL LIFE AND OTHER STORIES

# A Parallel Life

## I

"WE DON'T GET the lives we want," he said, rolling over, giving me his pitted shoulders to stare at and reaching for a cigarette.

"No smoking," I said. "You smokers don't know how the smell hangs on. The stink will outlive you. He'll know in a second that someone was here."

"Doesn't he have some idea?" He dropped the package of cigarettes and rolled back over to look at me. He had a large forehead from which his crinkly black hair seemed to have shrunk and protruding, practically pupilless eyes that were almost the same color as his hair.

"Of course not," I said pulling up the covers. I wasn't modest but the room was cool—chilly really. "You're right about not getting the lives we want. We're expected to choose before we know who we are."

"Exactly. And because we made certain choices before we knew what life was all about, this is what we wind up doing."

"Well, at least we get this," I said, turning away, not wanting to let him slide into some desultory song and dance. "There are a lot that don't."

"Won't. My wife for one." He picked up his watch from the nightstand. "God, I'd wish she'd cheat." Then he stood up and began to dress, first putting on his shirt, next his tie, and I was left lying on my new sheets, 230 threads per inch, feeling not desultory, but sad—the way I always did after I made love to a man who wasn't my husband.

I told myself that I could take credit for not lying. I never said that I did what I did because my husband didn't love me. That's not the way it was. He did. And I loved him in return. And I didn't love the man I was with. I refused to be sentimental, to invent a romance to excuse myself. There was nothing wrong about my life with Bill. I didn't look for love. I understood what Jack meant. We wanted more than we felt was allowed. We were restless and curious. I had no quibbles with the concept of monogamy. It just hadn't been enough for me.

So while Jack Duggan pulled on his trousers and I slid on my pantyhose, I didn't have any particular expectations about the way things might go. I didn't know then that in eight months I'd be stumbling out of a room leaving Jack Duggan inside pounding on walls and wailing. I couldn't have foreseen then that in eight months I'd be so filled with despair and sorrow that I was sure if I spent even five more minutes with Jack I'd sink into a darkness so profound that I'd never swim out.

I'd liked Jack from the moment he edged around the browsing rack and into my view. I was happy to have him appear because it had been such a slow morning at the library. The most excitement so far had come from two street people having a race for a corner chair, which was best for dozing. The older man, a fellow named Burt who kept up appearances by always wearing a tie, won. He'd celebrated his victory by falling asleep immediately and letting small gruntlike snores escape. More excitement arrived when my supervisor passed by with a memo on new rules for the use of the refrigerator in the staff room.

I could tell right away that Jack was not a man who knew his way around a library, but he was also a man who hated to appear as if he wasn't in control of a situation. First he flipped through the records, then he took magazines from the periodicals rack, then he eyed a display on local history. His face was square and candid, and his eyes did very quick takes, almost as if he was snapping photos for future use.

"I had no idea all of this was here," he whispered, leaning over, both elbows on my counter, and smiling to show me how much he approved. He had a gap between his front teeth, something I've always found appealing.

"You don't have to whisper," I said.

"No?" He looked surprised. Then he tilted his head slightly so that my eyes would have to meet his. "But I like to whisper."

His son had a report to write on some aspect of World War I, and Jack had decided that the boy should do it on the fighter planes of that period. I led Jack to the right section. Air Battles are catalogued by the Dewey decimal system at 940.4 and War Planes at 940.44. "It's all computerized today," he said, going to the shelf and running his fingers down the spine of a book. "War, video games, it's all the same. Where's the adventure? I want him to read about the real stuff."

I shrugged. He moved along the shelves pulling down one book, then another as he swaggered to compensate for a small limp. I decided that I had a fix on Jack already. He wore a raw silk jacket and linen slacks, a nice silk tie loosened at the throat, and good Italian loafers. He was a bit of a hustler, I decided, a man who liked the surface of things, a sentimentalist. He was vain and shallow, which would give me the liberty to despise him a little—a precaution against falling in love. But as I said, I liked him. He was open and he didn't take himself completely seriously.

We had lunch in a downtown restaurant that day. The next week I brought him to my house during my break. One of the best things about my job is that I have a four-hour break in the middle of the day. Contrary to what the movies would have you believe, most affairs—cheating, or whatever—go on during the day. People with families generally have to be home at night.

In the beginning, I'd told myself that Jack and I played by a set of mutually understood rules, and that we could leave our other lives on the floor with our clothes and climb into bed truly naked. I was wrong, of course. I'd assumed too much. I'd assumed that we could handle any situation. I'd assumed we understood consequences.

On the way out of the door of my house that first afternoon, I remember picking up a McCall's pattern from the kitchen counter. I was making a clown costume for my eight-year-old, Amy, for Halloween and hadn't bought enough material for the ruffled collar. Mandy, my eleven-year-old, was going out to trick-or-treat as a hobo. She had just reached the age at which she wanted to put together her own costume and I remember feeling a sense of loss as I stuffed the envelope into my handbag. I liked sewing for my daughters and I was going to miss it. I'd loved making frilly little-girl dresses, but as soon as they got into school neither wanted to wear anything except jeans and T-shirts like the other kids.

I got in my car and Jack sat in the passenger seat and ducked down as I opened the garage door with the remote. Driving up to the house or away from it with a guy crouched over so as not to be seen by the neighbors was so quintessentially slapstick that I almost always wound up giggling. It was always a relief to laugh about what we were doing because ultimately these afternoon liaisons struck me as pretty silly—lighthearted and insignificant ways to spend time. As I pressed on the gas, easing the car backward, Jack chuckled and inched his hand up under my skirt and gave me what felt like a fond pat on my inner thigh.

So Jack Duggan went back to his insurance office and I went back to the reference desk. It's funny how much I like the job—how much I like knowing where I'll be able to find out what comet it was that some kid in junior high saw with a telescope at two in the morning, or what the cost of chicken feed was in Duluth, Minnesota, on April 15, 1911.

I'd known that Jack was married. When he'd come into the library to find books on World War I planes, he was wearing a ring. Well, so what? I was married too. I wore a ring. Soon, with Jack, as with the others, we wound up talking about our spouses. It was a pretty safe thing to talk about—spouses, kids, or ex-spouses, if there were any. There was always an understanding that there wouldn't be any future for the "us" thing. Sometimes there'd be plans for a weekend somewhere—up on the coast or to the Sierras or Tahoe— but those weekends usually involved too many variables. Weekends away were a risk to the affair. We weren't kids, after all, trying to find out how it would feel to be married.

Little by little I heard about his wife, Roxie. A funny name. He told the story they all tell. Roxie didn't really like sex. They slept together, but if he would so much as touch her, she'd move away and make growling noises. It was funny, of course, to picture him reaching out and her growling—funny if I didn't allow myself to think about it.

I'd done the same thing to Bill. I'd pulled away from his touches, pretended to be asleep, added an extra couple of days to my period. I don't know why. I loved Bill. I even liked him. I liked the way he smelled. I liked his sweetness, his ability to be patient with my mother's tirades, his gentleness with the girls, his ability to handle a hard job and not take out his stress on me.

Jack sold insurance. He'd gone to City College and taken business courses. He'd been struck by a car when he was fourteen and his knee was smashed into a pulp that even the best surgery wasn't able to restore completely, so although most of his friends tried to avoid the draft and Vietnam, Jack felt that he was being kept out of something grand and glorious. He saw himself as an exile at home. His mother's brother had recognized Jack as a natural salesman and given him a job in his insurance firm. Jack turned out to be a very good salesman indeed, and with a fair amount of money coming in, Jack married —but not Roxie. He'd married a neighborhood girl. Even though they lived only blocks away from the Haight Ashbury district with its hippies and drugs and casual sex, Jack and Brigit were both virgins at the altar. Lots of things went wrong in the marriage and six months later they'd separated. Eight years after that, he met Roxie.

He was surprised when she agreed to marry him because he truly believed she was much too good for him. Roxie had finished Stanford, and in his words, "Roxie had a lot of class." Roxie taught fourth grade and he was proud of her. She'd been voted the best teacher in the Walnut Grove Unified School District. Her father was a doctor. He hadn't wanted Roxie to marry Jack, whose father worked in a brewery. Roxie had had three miscarriages before they'd been able to have little Jack and then little Annie. Roxie was delicate. Roxie liked nice things. Sometimes it drove him nuts the way she was so particular about the house. She had a nice body but she didn't like him looking at it. She wouldn't go down on him. But she loved him. And he loved her.

"I ask myself over and over why I do this," he said, raising his foot and touching my right nipple with his big toe. We sat facing each other in the Jacuzzi in one of Jack's friend's places in a big condo complex close to downtown —convenient for us both. Jack received a key in exchange for being able to get the friend off of an assigned risk policy after a drunk-driving arrest.

"You think I haven't wondered about it myself," I said. I was getting antsy. I had to be back at work in half an hour. My hair was wet and I'd forgotten to bring a dryer. "I look at it this way. I have affairs on my lunch break because I can take only so much of sitting around with my colleagues talking about wallpaper for the kitchen, menopause, or who's getting the best assignments."

"I'm serious," he said. "Do you think this is the sign of insanity? Why is it that I'll see a woman and be drawn to her so much I'll do anything to get to know her? Like you. I liked the way your glasses slipped down your nose and the way you kept pushing them up. I loved the inside of your hand. It looked so soft that I wanted to touch it. And you were wearing that plaid skirt. It was such an ugly skirt that it made me want you just like I'd want girls in high school when they wore those ugly plaid skirts."

"I don't want to think about it. I just accept it." I eased out and sat on the rim. He slid his hand over my wet ass and down to my knee. "I have important things to decide this afternoon. We're all chipping in for Shelly Novack's baby shower. Would you get her a playpen or a high chair?"

"We could just be friends, you and I," he said. "We'd have coffee downtown from time to time. Maybe a lunch. A walk by the creek in the park."

I wrapped a towel around myself. The Jacuzzi was on a ridiculous little deck with a view—if we wanted to open the louvers—of the county administration center, built in the fifties, and the new jail, a Postmodern version of an Art Deco version of something Assyrian. "I don't want to be just friends." I ran my hand through his hair and lifted it. It was thin but so lacquered it stayed up. "When you decide to be just friends, I'll find someone else."

He sighed and closed his eyes. He wanted me to feel sorry for him—for us. I went into the bedroom and began to dress. Maybe my hair would be almost dry by the time I got to work. I ran a comb through it and rubbed it with a towel and combed it again, ignoring the mirror. My hair was curly and I wore it short, the perfect hair for someone who's not going to be able to keep her head off pillows in the middle of the day. It was easy to resist looking at myself in the mirror. I was thirty-nine and the wrinkles had landed and were charting their territory. I had never been a beauty but I had decent features and good teeth in a pleasant, slightly too-long face. I looked like everyone's sister's best friend.

"We're good together," he said, coming up behind me and putting his nose in my damp hair. I could feel his cock against me.

We were, too. Better than I'd expected. When we made

love the very first time everything worked like gears meshing neatly. With Bill there were always problems now—mostly mine. I can find no fault with Bill. He's a better lover than most of the men I messed around with. In fact, I can say from some experience that men who mess around are usually not great lovers. The great lovers are men who love—not the performers who have all the tricks. And Bill loved me. He really did. I loved Bill. I had trouble desiring him. Maybe you can only desire what you don't have.

In high school the nuns told us that it was our obligation to make love to our husbands, that we should never refuse them. I reached up and pulled Jack's head against my neck. He licked the spot beneath my ear and I turned and pushed him away, my hand squarely on his bare chest. "Back off." He laughed and raised his hands in surrender. The ease of this was good.

That was late October. After some long pleasant November days, a bad winter began. On Thanksgiving, Bill came down with bronchitis that lingered until Christmas, and then right after New Year's, Amy hit a curb on her new bike and fell and broke her arm. While waiting outside the X-ray room in the hospital, I ran into Jonah coming out of the elevator.

I'd met Jonah at his garage sale two years ago. I was looking for an Exercycle for Bill. As I drove up, a young couple were loading a sofa onto the back of their pickup. "I just sold the love seat to that an hour earlier," he said, trying to laugh. He was a tall overweight young man with a jerkiness to his gestures caused not by palsy but nervousness.

The garage was practically empty. Bolt-together metal

shelves held a few quarts of motor oil and nothing else. Jonah scanned the space like a man peering into the water for some sign of bubbles from objects that had just disappeared from view.

"Give me a good price on the Exercycle and you can close shop."

"Twenty bucks," he said quickly, as if it were something he'd be glad not to have to deal with again.

"Sold." I opened my handbag.

He seemed surprised. "It needs a new chain."

"My husband's handy," I said.

"Some are." He turned away from me. Both the washer and dryer were disconnected and pulled from the wall. A dusty crew sock hung from the cold tap. "I guess I'm done."

I handed him two tens and smiled my best-friend smile and then decided he didn't need a best friend. I looked up and, as they say, established eye contact. It took him a minute or two to decide what to do as he folded and refolded the tens. "I've got some cold beer in the fridge," he said finally, checking up and down the empty street.

"Sounds good." I followed him into the garage and he lowered the door. In the kitchen we sat on the floor and drank a couple of supermarket-brand beers. Next, on a mattress on the floor in a bedroom surrounded by overflowing cardboard boxes, we made love—very nicely. Then he sobbed and showed me a stuffed bear he'd been sleeping with since his wife left.

I saw him maybe a dozen times after that. I helped him set up the kitchen in his new apartment and then I said good-bye for good. He was beginning to think something real was going on.

"Jonah," I said, dropping an empty diet Coke can into the trash.

"Ellen?" He still looked nervous, but he'd lost weight. Maybe he had a girlfriend. I hoped so. We caught up quickly. His mother had had surgery, an aneurysm repair, that morning. She was doing well. I told him about Amy's fall. It struck me that he didn't seem to have realized back then that I had children. When the orthopedic surgeon came over to tell me about Amy's X-rays, Jonah blushed and took two steps backward and bumped into a gurney.

Her break wasn't simple. Her arm had somehow twisted in the fall and the fracture had spiraled. They wanted to keep her until the next day. I spent the night in a chair at her side. In the dim room with the monitor lights colored like those on the Christmas tree still standing in the corner of our living room, Amy rode her bed gallantly like a small traveler on a space ship. From time to time I got up and placed my cheek against her narrow chest to feel it swell, its twin balloon lungs unfailing beneath ribs fragile as a bird's.

At dawn, Bill, looking pale—still not completely well, arrived to relieve me. I lifted my head and breathed foul overnight hospital breath in his direction as he bent to kiss me. He was a lovely man and his presence made me glad. I'd been dreaming about getting naked into a yellow taxi with Jack, who was wearing an overcoat from which his own bare legs stretched.

Because of someone's vacation, I found myself spending the next two weeks working afternoons and evenings with only a one-hour break from four to five. Mornings

were Jack's busy time so we had to struggle to get together
—still we managed at least twice a week between eleven
and one when I began work. In the middle of January,
Mr. Boudreau, my mother's landlord, phoned me from
Oakland to tell me that she had started screaming at the
other tenants again. I took off a day and drove down to
her apartment, a pleasant sunny place only a block from
Lake Merritt. She didn't want to let me in, but I talked
her into slipping the chain.

"You're here because he called you, but I can tell you
that I don't need admonishing," she said, turning her
back to me and walking into the kitchen. I smelled burnt
coffee. Her muttering rose and fell as she turned off the
gas and poured coffee into the cup. She managed to
sound like those messages over the loudspeakers in air-
ports from which only an occasional word is intelligible.
"Sugar," I heard her say, then "outlaw," then "cockroach."

"Mother." I touched her shoulder. She ignored my
hand. "Mother, you're not taking your medicine."

"The hell with that damn medicine," she said, pouring
milk into the cup and stirring it as she turned to face me.
She was sixty-four and still trim—a fading blonde with
blue eyes that seemed to capture and hold light. She'd
been beautiful. Her wedding picture could still take my
breath away. In it, she rose from swirls of satin as if
emerging from a shell. Her right hand rested inside the
grip of my father, who managed, despite his navy lieu-
tenant's uniform, to look like a rogue. "You and your sister
—neither one gives a damn about me. I don't know why I
let you in. You're Little Miss Fine and Dandy, and all
you've ever thought about is yourself."

"I think you should let me find you a place close by me
so I can check on you."

"The cockroaches are terrible here, but do you care? They talk to each other. They'll be here when we're all gone. When we're all in hell, they'll be strutting around. La-de-dah."

"There are some very nice apartments only a few blocks away from my house. You could walk to the stores. The girls could drop in on you and run errands for you."

"Your father was a bastard and you're his daughter, and your daughters will wind up riding off on the backs of motorcycles."

"You should be taking your pills," I said. "There's no need for you to get so agitated." She turned away as if I wasn't there and began to mutter again, her voice rising and falling in pitch, doppplering in and out of my consciousness.

I checked through her trash and then brought it down to the dumpster. I pulled down all the bottles in her medicine cabinet. Then I examined the linen closet. She'd emptied the pill bottle into an old bath-salts jar, where the tiny tablets lay half dissolved in some sort of liquid. Shampoo? I phoned her doctor and asked for more. I told him she was having a rough time. He said he'd raise the dosage but there was nothing he could do if she didn't take them. Of course not. I got her into the car and drove to the drugstore where I picked up the prescription and bought her magazines—*Vogue* and *Bazaar*—and a Coke and watched her take the pill. Then we drove up to Tilden Park, where we could look down on the blue stretches of the bay with the winter-green land rising from it. She stopped muttering and leaned back, closing her eyes. If only someone had nothing to do but drive her around.

We went to a Chinese restaurant downtown. She used a fork and hurried food into her mouth as if she were starving. I ordered beef and vegetables to take back. She'd never liked to cook. Her freezer was stuffed with TV dinners.

I took off the next day too and called Jack. We drove to the coast in Jack's car and walked on the beach. January can be the kindest time at the coast. We sat against sun-warmed rock and watched the seals crawl up onto the sand. I tried to talk to Jack about my mother's problems, but he gave back only the most perfunctory comments, which made me angry with myself. He was smarting from some social insult by a client who hadn't asked him to a cocktail party at the country club. I wondered why I was trying to talk to Jack when Bill understood every-thing so well and usually could make me feel better.

We went to a motel and drank Irish whiskey in bed in a room with gold-flecked wallpaper and a purple carpet. As if to make up for having been so distant on the beach, Jack made love actively, but it felt forced and I didn't have an orgasm, which he decided to take as an affront.

Now that I look back on that time, I wonder how our affair lasted as long as it did. Even though I liked him, almost everything Jack did struck me as wrong headed or pathetic. He harbored relentless social ambitions. He bragged about how he'd gotten the best of almost every-one. He was a gun notcher. A keeper of scores. He wore chattery sports jackets and a gargantuan class ring. He drove a Mazda RX. JAX RX said the plates. He really wanted a Porsche. He thought of Las Vegas as a vacation possibility. We h..d nothing in common but our time together and a certain bald lust. I had a list made up of things to hold against him. He was uneducated, he had lousy taste in clothes, and he cheated on his wife.

"I'm going to be busy this next week," I said as I got out in front of a vacant storefront around the corner from the library and emptied sand from the pocket of my jacket.

"Me too," he said and screeched away from the curb without looking back.

The following Friday my mother called. In a calm voice she told me that she had started saying the rosary. "I began on Tuesday with the Sorrowful Mysteries. I know you're supposed to alternate with the Joyful and Glorious Mysteries, but I just don't feel like them right now. I pray every evening right after the ten o'clock news."

I told Bill about this latest development. "That's very sane," he said. "Maybe we should all pray after the ten o'clock news."

"But you don't believe in God," I said. "You could only pray ironically." He was a mathematician who spent his days writing instructions for computers. His atheism had been a most attractive quality to me when I'd met him in Berkeley. His walk across the paving of Sproul Plaza had possessed a buoyancy that I attributed to a freedom from a belief in original sin. He hadn't thought of himself as stained from the start. He'd been a dangerously thin, fair-haired young man from the Midwest preoccupied with learning, and he seemed uncomplicated in ways I had not believed possible.

"That's not true," he said. "Not believing in God doesn't mean I don't believe in prayer." He pulled me into the hollows of his curled-up body. He held me, his arms crossed in front of my chest to protect me. His kindness and optimism were enormous.

A fact that never ceased to fascinate me is that Bill suspected nothing about my other men. He had never once asked me to account for my time away from him. He'd had one affair. I knew he'd been with someone else the moment he began to make love to me after getting home from the convention. There was a new sort of exactness to his caress—tentative, almost pedantic—as if he'd just learned a new formula and was anxious to apply it. I found the strangeness exciting. I also knew that he'd tell me about her. He did. A month later. She lived in Los Angeles and she'd just gotten divorced. He'd had too much to drink, and so on. She told him that she'd been so lonely she'd put an ad in the personals.

I never understood why people needed the personals in the newspaper. Jack and I had found each other in the library without any help from the Dewey decimal system. We could have been wearing cards. *Married. Unfaithful but discreet.* I'd never had a problem locating lovers. People like Jack and me form a substantial underground— a fellowship like the Masons or the Elks. And we don't even need a special handshake or meetings to recognize one another. When Jack asked me for lunch, I'd known what would follow. Bill did not belong to that fellowship. His affair was an accident, a freak. He didn't even know the fellowship existed.

I'd already had half a dozen lovers by Bill's first affair, and the fact that I became aware at once of his affair made me wonder why he'd never appeared to notice when I'd been with someone else. Perhaps he told himself that my occasional requests for something new, for a variation on the immutability of our routine, was the result of research—something I'd come across at the reference desk. It never occurred to Bill that I might be who I was. It had never occurred to Bill that I might have a parallel life.

I woke up in the middle of that night to a vision of my

mother on her knees in front of the dark television set
pulling the beads one by one through her long pale fingers.
I saw the brown-speckled backs of her hands. I saw the
cross swaying like a pendulum as her fingers rubbed the
faceted crystal surfaces, releasing from the fastness of each
set of stones its store of devotion to the terrible—the agony,
the scourging, the thorns, the burden, the crucifixion and
death. My heart pounded and my mouth went dry. Bill
lay beside me sucking air in ragged gulps between snores.

My split shift was restored to me. Amy's bone knit.
Bill began to jog in the mornings before work. Mandy
acquired a boyfriend who collected stamps. She asked me
to bring home books on stamps so she could know what
to talk to him about. We got record rainfall.

When, after a couple of weeks, Jack called and asked if
I wanted to see him, I said yes. Jack's friend had had the
walls of his rooms painted a pale, hard gray. According to
Jack, his friend now had a girlfriend and she was redeco-
rating for him. There was a new black-leather sofa, a
chrome-and-glass table with chrome-and-leather chairs.
We now made love on gray-and-red plaid designer sheets.
Jack's friend hadn't told his girlfriend about our using the
place. We were pleased by that. As we drained the cham-
pagne from a bottle in the refrigerator and finished the
Brie, we smiled. The chance to assume the role of inter-
lopers honed a new edge on the afternoon.

The days away from Jack had given me time to want
him again. On the night before Jack called, I'd made love
to Bill for the first time in weeks—and it had been
astonishingly good. Missing Jack allowed me to succumb
to Bill's tenderness, and Bill's tenderness had made me
wake up hungry for Jack's urgency, for Jack's ability to

forget I was there—so that I could get lost too—so that I could savor sex without a relationship attached to it.

Jack's friend's girlfriend had left a hair dryer on the bathroom counter, so I washed my hair in the shower. When I came back into the bedroom, Jack was still in bed. He'd turned on the television and was watching a soap. There's something too quiet about soaps. There's almost no modulation in the voices even though dreadful things are supposed to be happening to the characters.

"These shows make me uneasy," I said, pushing aside a heart-shaped box of chocolates. It was Valentine's Day and Jack had presented me with the box right before we began making love. I'd laughed. It had seemed a sweet and slightly campy thing for him to do. We'd eaten chocolates, swapping fillings as we kissed. Now I put the lid on the box and slipped on my blouse.

"Me too." He swung his legs over the edge and sat hands on knees. "I don't know why I turned it on."

"To watch adultery being sanctified by the networks."

He didn't seem to hear but kept his eyes on the screen. Two women, both blondes, looked back at us as if seeing us in the haze of a crystal ball. "My wife went to the doctor yesterday," he said after a moment. "She found a lump in her left breast."

I felt as if he'd hit me. "They're mostly benign," I said, catching my breath. "We just got a new report on breast lumps last week."

"She had a mammogram. There's something there. She's going in for a biopsy tomorrow."

"The prognosis for a cure with an early discovery is excellent," I said. I felt dizzy. "I keep up on it. We get so many calls."

"I guess you do." He sighed and stood and put on his shirt. "I'm trying not to worry."

"She'll be fine," I said as I tucked in my blouse. I wondered if I sounded convincing.

He walked around the bed and stood in front of me, his flaccid penis hanging between the tails of his open shirt. I placed my hand on his thigh, gently, non-erotically, the first stage of a pat. He bent and kissed the top of my head. "Thank you," he said.

"I'm sorry, Jack."

"I haven't touched her breasts in months," he said and turned, giving me his rear, and stepped into his shorts.

## II

The public library is right downtown. Walnut Grove is a moderate-sized California city in a coastal valley. A few years ago to counter the bloom of shopping centers on the outskirts, the city fathers redeveloped this part of town, which meant tearing down a lot of fine buildings and turning the old courthouse into the kind of mall where pricey little stores sell things that I can only imagine buying as wedding presents for someone I hardly know. But then I'm not a shopper. The former lawyers' offices and coffee shops are now restaurants and antiques stores. The winos who recently roamed this section had disappeared—rounded up and shot, for all I know.

After work, I had decided to walk to a candy store to buy Bill a box of chocolates. He'd be pleased, touched even. On my way I passed a bar that had once been the place where reporters hung out. Now the old plaster had been sandblasted away and the place was all rose-colored brick, brass, and indirect lighting. Its current owner staged a weekly lingerie show during happy hour. As I passed by the doors, the lingerie show had ended and people were leaving. Some stood, glowing with alcohol, just outside in the mild February evening.

Two men bracketed a woman beside the door. I saw her face, a flash of pink, between the backs of the men as I came closer and I could tell from the postures exactly what was going on. Each of the men was trying to win the woman for the rest of the evening. Seen from the rear, one of the two men struck me as a slightly taller and older version of Jack. He wore the same sort of sports coat Jack would choose, the same cut of slacks, the same kind of shoes, and he had the same expansive gestures and the same confiding hunch of the shoulders. As the man turned enough so that I could see his profile, I realized with a start that it was my father.

I veered and crossed the street, skirting a car backing into a parking space. I hadn't seen my father since Christmas eve when he'd come for dinner—my mother always came on Christmas day—bringing his latest girlfriend, a listless woman, younger than me, who was a secretary at the Chrysler dealership where he was in his own evaluation "the top man on the floor." My father is shameless and I didn't want to have to run into him on the street and endure his glib patter intended to disguise the fact that I had come upon him outside a bar trying to score.

He left us when I was ten and my sister, Maureen, was twelve. I know that he would say that he didn't leave us, that he left our mother, but Maureen and I had a hard time not feeling that we shared our mother's fate—which seemed not like a fate then but a punishment. All three of us had done something wrong and all three of us were being banished for misdeeds—only we stayed and he was the one who was gone.

Not that he'd ever been around all that often. Even then he was "in sales" and a traveler. But when he was home, he was unmistakably there—a presence, a force—making jokes, flirting with me and Maureen, calling us his sweethearts, his true loves and then plunging into a sulk because no one appreciated him. During these times he would refuse to talk and my mother, as if he were deaf not dumb, would raise the pitch of everything she said, banging pots and pans onto the table for punctuation.

"You see how she drives me out of the house," he'd say, putting on his hat and jacket in the open door while the wind off the ocean pushed the fog into the room.

We lived in San Francisco then in the Richmond district on the bottom floor of one of those countless pallid houses, proper and domestic, in which our kind of people lived. Jack Duggan had grown up not far away. Four years older than me, he'd gone to the same high school as my boy cousins, and this evening I'd thought of him when I'd seen my father's back.

My hand was shaking as I handed the woman in the tidy white dress the twenty-dollar bill and it shook as I took the red heart-shaped box from her in the shop smelling of chocolate. There was a crush of people. I wondered how many of those waiting on the black-and-white tiles for their numbers to be called were like me—like Jack Duggan. I wondered how many heart-shaped boxes my father had bought that day.

Bill sat on a stool in the kitchen watching basketball on the small television. He grinned when I pulled the box of candy from the large canvas book sack I carry. Bill and I had made a pact a long time ago not to honor public holidays, and here I was breaking the rules. I could tell he was delighted. I let him kiss me, holding me against the refrigerator, tilting up my head, and sliding his tongue between my teeth. His lips went along my chin, down my neck. I felt his erection growing as he pressed against me and I wondered if my father had ever wanted to cry at times like this.

"The nets are too low," I said.

"Ummmh?"

"Basketball." I gently pushed him away. "I don't get basketball anymore."

We drank vodka and orange juice at the round glass table overlooking the Jacuzzi, which overlooked the county administration center. We hadn't touched each other yet. Jack was pale. He mixed the first drink and swallowed it in the kitchen, then he mixed another for himself and one for me. I hadn't had lunch. I sliced through yesterday's French bread that sat on the table. Outside, the rain turned the mountains into smudges.

"The doctor went into her armpit and took a sample of the nodes there," he said. "He found cancer in her lymph system. She's at what they call Stage Four. They're going to remove the breast tomorrow and then we'll see what the next treatments are."

"It's really bad then?"

He finished the drink and got up and walked to the sliding glass door. "It's not good." He banged his fist on the wall. "I don't know why the hell she waited so long."

"She'd known it was there?"

"Yes." He banged again. The framed Georgia O'Keeffe poster of the interior of a calla lily tilted over the leather couch. "Yes, yes, yes. She's not talking about it to me but she's known for a while. That's what the doctor told me when he called me at work. She'd been feeling it there for months, running her fingers over it—fondling it."

"What would you like us to do?" I chewed the bread but it wouldn't go down my throat.

He turned to me, surprised, and didn't answer.

"I mean do you want to keep this up—what we're doing—seeing each other?" It was obvious that this hadn't occurred to him yet. It was as if I had become, like his job, another part of his life. My stomach knotted.

"Of course," he said. "Sure."

"Fine." I went to the bedroom and took off my clothes and got under the sheets, but he didn't follow as he usually did. I waited, stretching under the sheets, lifting the comforter with my toes. The room seemed wet, as if the rain had found its way in. The sheets clung heavily, weighted with dampness. After a few moments, he came in and sat on the bed. "I can't right now," he said. "I want to but I can't right now."

"I understand." I pulled the sheet up to my chin and lay like a mummy. I'd never felt so naked. He put his hand on my shoulder as if I were the one who was ill, as if I were Roxie. I wanted to shrug off his hand. I wanted him to go away. I wanted more than anything to get dressed alone and leave by myself.

"Oh, Jesus," he said, letting out a breath. "*I* don't even understand." He gripped my shoulder harder. I pulled from his grip, turned back the sheet, and moved to make room for him. He lowered himself and lay down without even taking off his shoes. Neither of us moved until the alarm that we set to remind us that we had lives to return to began to buzz.

He called me at work the next morning and said he wanted to see me at lunch. We met outside the condominium door. He had trouble getting the key in the lock. His distress made him desperate. As soon as we were inside the door, he began to pull up my skirt. We made love not in bed but on the carpet in the living room with the draperies open and the louvers that protected the balcony from the eyes at the administration center open as well.

We continued after that, meeting two or three times a week for the next two months as if everything would go on as before, as if Roxie's crisis was happening in a foreign country and had nothing to do with us. And because Jack didn't mention her, I made an effort to put her out of my mind. Like an oyster with a grain of sand in its shell, I coated thoughts of Roxie with a glaze that hid her from my mind's eye. I made her existence easy to slip around.

Then I saw her. Walnut Grove just isn't big enough for these things never to occur. During my lunch break, I decided to go shopping. Mandy was going to be twelve soon and I wanted to find something for her. Bill had been a good tennis player when I'd met him and he and Mandy had begun playing last summer. With that in mind I thought I'd look for a decent tennis racquet for her, something better than the old wooden one she'd begun using as a beginner. I remembered a sporting goods store a few blocks from the library. It was one of several business in a small strip mall.

I remembered a pizza place there as well, and a laundromat, and a printing shop. I'd never noticed that one of the businesses was a wig shop until I saw Jack and a woman coming out of the door. The woman was tall, almost his height, and very thin. She wore checked slacks and a raincoat, and she had a flowered scarf tied babushka style around her head. Jack carried a round box, like a hat box. The woman clung to his arm and talked softly but with animation, using her eyebrows a great deal and nodding her scarf-covered head from one side to the other. She was a pretty woman and there was a certain tentative seductiveness in the nodding as if, though she knew she had once been found attractive, she was not sure if she could still be found so. Jack nodded in reply and gave her attention so complete that he failed to notice me standing stock-still in front of the window of the printing shop with its arrangement of pink-and-silver wedding invitations.

I kept my eyes on the display but watched him in the glass and saw his jolt of recognition as he looked my way. He made a swift recovery. Her back was to me and her monologue continued unbroken. She hadn't noticed. I heard the words *conference* and then *attendance records* and then a small chirrupy laugh that requested the listener's understanding and sympathy. He chuckled, three notes descending.

In the window glass I watched him help her down from the curb and open the door of a station wagon for her to get in on the passenger side. I watched until they were on the street. Then I went into the pizza place, which I knew would be dark and empty at that time of day, and ordered a large Coke, which, although I sat in the booth for over an hour, I never managed to drink.

In the library, I began my research. Stage Four meant that the cancer was advanced. Stage Four could mean that the tumors were over a certain size, or that the tumors had extended to the chest wall or the skin, or that there was evidence of cancer in the lymph nodes, or that there were distant metastases present. Or any combination of the above. None of these conditions held out much hope for an excellent prognosis.

Roxie, the woman in the scarf, the woman buying the wig, had no doubt already endured radiation, then chemotherapy. Both were awful treatments in which the patient was subjected to assaults that were only narrowly nonlethal. The success rates for all of these methods of treatments were displayed on the various pages as a smorgasbord of bar graphs and pie charts, all of which offered survival rates as percentages, degrees, and fractions.

Over the next few days, I read everything I could find on the subject and then tried to make myself forget what I had read. If Roxie had gone in as soon as she had found the lump, the buried deadliness, she'd have had great odds. But Roxie had waited and I didn't want to know her reasons. I only wanted Roxie to live—to recover. I wanted her to recover and Jack to fall in love with her all over again.

"She's just fine," he said when I asked about her the next day. It was the first time I'd brought her up since the day he lay fully clothed beside me. "The drugs made her hair fall out, but that's to be expected. It will grow back."

"What color hair does she have?" I was unable to control myself. I wasn't sure what I had felt when I saw them together but it was like the time Jonah had realized that I had a daughter. It's a device of self-protection to pretend that the other lives of people you're having affairs with are fictions. Before that day I had allowed myself to believe in Roxie's existence to the same extent that I believed in Moby Dick. Now she existed. She had brushed by me. I'd heard her laugh. I'd heard her suck air between words.

"It's a real honey blonde," he said. "Thick and blonde. It was the first thing I noticed about her. She was sitting at a table in a restaurant having lunch with a girlfriend and I couldn't take my eyes off her hair. It was long, almost to her waist. Of course, she's cut it since then." He rolled onto his back and stared at the ceiling as if watching a movie of Roxie's long blonde hair there. "The funny thing in the wig shop was that we couldn't decide what color wig to buy. She wanted to think about another color, you know. There was this long blonde wig and I wanted her to try it on but she wouldn't. I guess I understand that."

"It would be too close to what she'd lost."

"That's it. That's what I was thinking. But you know something very weird happened in there—something I wouldn't have expected."

I waited. I had, after all, asked the initial question.

"She tried on this dark wig—dark and wavy to her shoulders, and when she did she looked like herself and also like someone completely new at the same time. And I got aroused—right there in the store."

"Oh God," I said and rolled away from him. "Oh God."

"I know," he said, sitting up.

The apple tree in the backyard bloomed. The hillside at the end of our street flared with yellow mustard flowers. Amy's final cast came off. Mandy's twelfth birthday party was a success. Bill found a tennis racquet for her, and I bought her a sweater she'd admired that made her look like a small turtle in a very large shell. Amy gave her a Bon Jovi tape. My father came and brought a dozen pink roses and a gold chain necklace with a tiny diamond—her birthstone. The next day Bill went back east on business for two weeks and I missed him.

On the day after Bill left, I got a call at work from Jack. He and Roxie were flying to Miami to take a Caribbean cruise. It was something they'd always talked about but had never done. "The worst is over," he said. "She's on the mend."

I wanted to believe him. He said he'd call me when he got back.

I hung up and was surprised by how much relief I felt. I wouldn't see Jack again. I'd talk to him on the phone and tell him I was out of it. If he wanted to have an affair, he'd find someone—probably in a matter of hours. Ben Michaelsen, a co-worker, had been looking for someone to trade hours with so he could go back to school part-time. I'd give him my split shift. I'd go home at five each day and work in the yard. I'd buy seeds and compost and fertilizer and plant a vegetable garden. I'd be home in a kitchen redolent with spices, with the juices of simmering stews, with fruit in golden-crusted pies when Bill got home from work.

Mr. Boudreau called a few days later to tell me that my mother had slapped the cheek of the daughter of one of the other tenants in the front hallway of the building. According to the mother of the girl, my mother had come out into the hall to tell her that she played her stereo too loud. When the girl said she didn't think it was too loud, my mother called her a bitch. In return the girl called my mother a bitch and my mother slapped her.

"Your mother, she can be so sweet sometimes, but other times..." Mr. Boudreau let his voice drift off like a radio slipping out of range. "She always pays on time and I appreciate that but..."

"She's been there for years."

"I know..." He was waiting for me. I waited for him. "If she was my mother, I'd be worried..."

I was worried, I assured him. But she liked living there. I didn't want to relocate her against her will. I could see him shaking his head in agreement on the other end of the phone the way he always did, no matter what I said, whenever I spoke to him. I told him I'd drive down that evening.

My mother had moved to Oakland to be closer to her sister. When her sister died, my mother stayed on. Her sister, a religious woman who heard the litany of my mother's tribulations over and over again, had been her only real friend. "High strung," they'd once called people like my mother. "Nervy."

She'd always had a temper. She'd pulled our hair when we were girls. Slapped both of us. She threw things at my father. She had a bone to pick with the world and for this everyone suffered. She was angry, she was anxious, she was miserable. When my father had been there, she said he drove her crazy with his demands. When he was gone, she wailed because she'd been deserted. She used menopause as an excuse for more erratic behavior for the next fifteen years. Bill had me take her to a doctor, then a psychiatrist. Both were vague. The psychiatrist prescribed tranquilizers. She'd take them for a while and then decide that they were destroying her—and in a way she was right. She was an angry woman—not a tranquil one. She felt like a traitor to herself when she wasn't filled with rage.

She let me in without any problems this time, but she wouldn't speak. I followed her into the kitchen where she sat and stabbed a fork into some brownish mess sitting in an aluminum tray—Salisbury steak?—forked a piece into her mouth and began to chew, scowling as her jaws ground the meat into paste.

"I've had a bad report," I said, sitting opposite and feeling foolish and resentful for having to behave like a principal. "I understand you slapped the girl from the apartment upstairs."

She laughed, a sharp barking sound. "She had it coming. She's a slut. You should see her. If one of your daughters dressed like that you'd lock her up."

"You can't slap people. It's called assault. They could have you arrested. *You* could be locked up."

She kept chewing and didn't answer. I don't think she's ever enjoyed food. She always acted as if eating was a contest of wills between herself and whatever was on her plate. When the aluminum compartments were empty, she jerked open the garbage can and dumped the tray and then threw the fork into the sink. "Go to jail. That's what you'd love. To see me in jail. Then I'd be taken care of—out of your hair."

"You're going to have to move, Mother. I'm going to find you a place close to me. In the meantime, you have to take your pills."

"The hell with the pills."

The bottle sat on the table by the salt and pepper. I shook a pill into the palm of my hand, filled a glass with water, and offered them both to her.

"The hell with you," she said, but she took them.

I made us each a cup of tea and sat with her through

"Nova," watching naked people in a rain forest hunt parrots and devour large white grubs found inside of dead trees. "Delicious," my mother said, which I took as a good sign. "Time for the news," she said when "Nova" was over.

"Are you still praying the rosary after the news?" I asked as I got up to leave.

"For me to know and you to find out," she said.

That night I dreamed that my mother was having a garage sale and that Roxie came and bought all of my mother's sheets and blankets. I woke up in a sweat.

For the first time since I'd learned of Roxie's illness, I forced myself to explore the territory of my breasts. I placed my right arm behind my head and checked first the right breast, my fingers flat like a spatula, pressing gently. Then with the left arm behind my head, I checked the left breast. My left breast was larger than the right, although both were smallish. Throughout high school, my inability to achieve cleavage had seemed like a curse, but lately I'd been happy with my breasts. Smallish, they resisted sagging. I placed the pads of my fingers on the density of the fibrous tissue under the skin and moved it gently. I squeezed my nipple and thought of my mother. If my mother felt she betrayed herself by accepting tranquility, did I feel that to refrain from affairs would be a betrayal of some desperate concept I had of myself? And what would Roxie want with my mother's bedding?

I now spent my breaks on an apartment search. On the third day, I saw a place on the ground floor in an older but well-maintained building. It had a small patio and long windows facing south. The rent was quite a bit less than my mother was paying in Oakland. I wrote a check for a deposit and told the manager I'd be back with my mother on the first of the month. The building was on my way to work and I could stop by every morning to check on her. Each apartment had a separate entrance off a brick walkway. There was no hall for her to stand in to yell at the other tenants. Perhaps a change in architecture would encourage a change in behavior.

I missed Bill. Not horribly, but mildly. I tried not to think of Jack, but that was difficult. If I thought of him, I'd remember the way Roxie had passed by. I'd remember the maze of the flowers on her scarf reflected in the window, her voice, her box carried by Jack. Two days before Bill was to get back, I decided to call Jonah.

Jonah was a CPA in an office where he was constantly scrutinized by his boss. In the past, however, he'd managed to find time for me during the day. Jonah wasn't Jack. He wasn't really an adulterer. He was a lonely guy who just happened to get found by a woman. When I called Jonah, I told myself that I had really nothing in mind—no agenda—that I merely wanted to see him, to have lunch, to find out how he was getting along.

Jonah sounded guarded on the phone but he named a Mexican restaurant a few blocks from the library on the west side of town near the railroad tracks, a real Mexican place with good food. I decided to walk. This whole valley had once been planted in orchards, and in vacant lots and behind old buildings, fruit trees could still arrest passersby with the sudden cloudy voluptuousness of their blooming. As if born out of those same flowers, bees now appeared in my path, swirling around errant boughs reaching over the sidewalk. Green shoots widened the cracks in the pavement and petals torn down by last night's rain filled the gutters. Because of the beauty of the day, I decided that I didn't need to make resolutions about anything. I decided that to believe I could resolve anything would be an act of audacity. Life, I decided, had its own rhythms and patterns and to abandon myself to these was the greatest wisdom.

Jonah had a cold—or maybe it was hay fever. His eyes watered and he blew his nose constantly. I couldn't believe he'd chosen a Mexican restaurant on top of this distress, but perhaps some homeopathic reasoning lay at the heart of it, a belief that like heals like, and making your eyes and nose run by eating hot sauce would cure a cold.

"I think about you a lot," he said. He'd ordered a beer and it rested in a chilled mug in front of him. "More than a lot." He looked down into the beer as soon as he'd spoken.

"Well, I think about you too," I said. I immediately regretted having called him. He wasn't a player. He was for real in the way that Bill was for real. "I wondered if you'd found somebody."

"I was seeing a woman for a while, but it didn't work out." He blew his nose into a large handkerchief with a wet morose sound. "I wish you could have stayed around."

A waiter arrived with chips and guacamole and salsa. I ordered a beer. "Well, I'm married, Jonah, and I couldn't allow myself to get serious. But I like you. It was nice making love to you."

"Better than nice," he said.

"It was nice for me because it was supposed to be fun. I didn't want it to go anywhere. It wasn't supposed to become a courtship."

"You believe that, don't you?"

"Yes. I don't think good sex and a good relationship are Siamese twins. You don't get one with the other necessarily."

"You're sick," he said, sounding immensely dismal for my sake.

"Maybe so, Jonah. I just don't take what we did that seriously."

"Well, I still want to sleep with you." He stabbed the guacamole with the chip.

"I still want to sleep with you too, but that's not why I called." If I had when I'd called, I didn't any longer. I stabbed my own chip into the gaucamole. It would be a long lunch. "It's hard to find a good relationship, but it's worth it—even if the sex isn't the greatest. You have to try not to get discouraged."

He loosened his tie. He'd gained weight again. He wiped his eyes.

I invited my father for dinner. I wanted to warn him that I was moving my mother to town. Despite the fact that they'd been separated for almost thirty years and divorced for twenty-six, my mother still called him from time to time whenever she felt a need to lay her misery on his doorstep. I'd heard both ends of these conversations and I'd been on both sides. My father had moved up here after Bill and I had, not to be nearer us, but because one of his girlfriends lived here. He hadn't married her, but he had married someone else later on who also lived in town. After they'd divorced, he'd stayed, claiming he'd lost his taste for the city. That night, my father arrived with a bottle of very good cabernet sauvignon and a bouquet of irises.

I placed the irises in a tall vase while Mandy lit candles

for the table, which she had set with the good china and silver. This seemed excessively elegant to me for a dinner of deli ravioli and salad, but both of my daughters responded to their grandfather much as Maureen and I had, and there seemed no way that I could change that. Richard Kellerher was a romantic and enigmatic figure, always impeccably dressed, charming, and polite. They were too young for me to tell them that he was a heartbreaker—an untrustworthy and duplicitous person.

He flattered my daughters as no one else did. He noticed what they wore, when they changed hairstyles. He paid for Mandy to have riding lessons, for Amy to take ballet. Amy was less susceptible to his charms than Mandy, but only because she was more self-absorbed and less susceptible to everything. For this reason, he wooed her even more. "Let me see that arm," he asked as she set the plates around the table.

She had been self-conscious when the cast came off. "There was all this old scaly skin at first," she said. "It looked like a dinosaur arm."

"Ah," he said, holding it between his hands and examining it. "I can't believe that. Now it looks like something carved from precious ivory."

"That's silly, Grandpa," she said, giggling.

"No. It's a treasure that has been sealed away and is now revealed."

She giggled again and rolled her eyes in my direction.

"It's skinnier than the other," said Mandy. "Amy should lift weights."

"Not too many weights," he said shuddering. "Girls shouldn't look like boys."

"I'm going to lift weights," said Mandy, studying him for a reaction. "But just enough."

After dinner, I made him come into the kitchen as I loaded the dishwasher. It would never have occurred to him to help clear the table. "I've found Mother a place close by," I said. "So I can keep track of her. I'll check on her every day."

"Why is it that no one checks on me every day?"

"Because you don't need it."

"There's nothing wrong with her, you know." He sat on a high stool and crossed his legs almost primly. I'd noticed the same occasional primness in Jack. "She just likes to annoy people. She's extremely dramatic."

"She doesn't make anyone nearly as unhappy as she makes herself."

"I know," he sighed. "Do I have to suffer her? I hope she doesn't expect to see me. She can't seem to understand what divorce means."

"She doesn't believe in it. You know that. But I doubt that she'll turn up at your door and harangue you."

"I'm seeing other women, you know."

"When haven't you?"

He chuckled and looked smug. "Very good. When haven't I?"

"The one you brought on Christmas eve?"

"No. She was too young. Someone nearer to my age."

"I guess that's a good thing." I closed the dishwasher and turned the knob.

"You women have it made nowadays," he said as the machine began to hum.

"She'll phone you."

"I have never deserted your mother, despite what she likes to believe," he said and recrossed his legs. "Never."

On Saturday, Bill drove a rented U-Haul down to Oakland where Mr. Boudreau supplied his nephew Calvin to help us load my mother's things into the truck in order to hasten the departure of his troublesome tenant. Calvin was a surly young man with a shaved head and extremely expensive sneakers who sneered at each box he carried to the U-Haul. I'd come down the day before to help Mother pack, to wrap glasses in newspapers, and sort things for Goodwill. In anticipation of some fit of anger or intransigence, I'd made sure that she had taken her pills, but she seemed positively cheerful as the morning of the move arrived. Perhaps she enjoyed the attention, for she dawdled regally each time Calvin arrived to ask her which box was ready to go down next.

"Doesn't she realize I'm paying him by the hour?" Bill whispered to me as my mother took a set of plates out of one box and repacked them in an almost-identical manner in another while Calvin drummed on the refrigerator—which, thank God, belonged to his uncle and didn't have to be moved.

"She'll push it to the limit," I said, but Bill already knew this. He groaned loudly as he lifted a box of pots and pans and winked at me.

My mother ignored the groan and scowled at Calvin. "This is probably the most exercise you've had in years," she said.

His reaction to this was an uncontestable look of shock. I picked up a box and left the room. "Not exactly," I heard him say.

The early fog had evaporated and the morning was one of those fine ones in which the sun and the air seem to

combine so that the air shimmers and the light has sub-
stance. A breeze carried the scent of water in from the bay.
I followed Bill into the interior of the truck where he and
Calvin had already placed my mother's couch and easy
chair and dresser. I put down my box, pivoted him by his
shoulders, and pressed him against the upended mattress
and kissed him. He tasted salty with sweat from all the
lifting and stairs. "I love you," I said licking his unshaved
Saturday cheek. "I've never loved anyone but you."

"What's this all about?" He had wonderfully candid
eyes and talk of affection still embarrassed him, but he
put his arms around me.

"I missed you when you were gone."

He tightened his arms as I leaned against his chest,
pressing against him, glad for the comfort of his honest
body, happy to be found in those arms by Calvin a few
minutes later.

I am not ignorant of the fact that what Jack and I did is
the stuff that provides the grist for the mills of daytime
talk shows, radio call ins, and countless articles in all
kinds of journals. "What to do if your husband—or
wife—is unfaithful?" "Portrait of a cheater?" "Is infidelity
a disease?" "Is infidelity an addiction?" These banners lurk
in magazine racks as we wait for our groceries to be lifted
and weighed, scanned and paid for. It's as if these magazines also offered some sort of nourishment—bar-coded
as they are just like the cartons of cereal and bags of bread
and cans of beans.

I've read my share of articles. And yet none of them
really seems quite right when they try to explain infidelity. They all seem too complicated in a way and yet not
complicated enough.

I know my behavior runs the risk of putting the marriage in jeopardy, but affairs provide me with something no other activity seems to offer—and in a very brief, condensed amount of time. If it could be considered a hobby, it would occupy a great deal less time than most hobbies. I have a friend who figure-skates and is away from her family almost every evening and on many weekends when she goes to competitions. If you live in a big city, you could probably spend more time looking for a parking space than I spend in these trysts.

And it is precisely the matter of time that is important. Because of the very nature of an affair, because it must be covert, the time with a lover is limited. The time spent in an affair is also qualitatively as well as quantitatively different than times with a spouse. The time spent with a lover is analogous to the taste of a dried pear from which the tasteless water has evaporated so the gritty sweetness of the flesh is concentrated. Because an affair requires strategies and risks, the other person in that affair must be viewed as worthy of these efforts. It is the distance and obstacles between two people that create the conditions of desire. A person is desired because that person is not possessed.

When I'm meeting a lover, my heart does pound faster and therefore there is more blood circulating, and more oxygen is being carried to my lungs and brain. I am more alert. Smells, textures, tastes are all heightened. A sensory edge emerges that ordinary time dulls. The first encounter is always feral with its sniffing, touching, its dance of seduction. The very act of coming together involves immense delicacy and even wariness since the goal is to surprise but not startle. There is no map for this. I am going into new lands in which I need both the ability to rely on pure reflex and also to pay complete attention.

I have to lose myself and yet be present. Nothing else is so focused and also so expansive.

Although by my calendar calculations I reckoned that Jack must have returned from his cruise, I didn't hear from him. I told myself that this was fine, that I hadn't wanted to go on seeing Jack anyway, that I really wanted only Bill, that I was finally willing to settle into monogamy. I warned myself that sooner or later Bill would discover what I had been up to. I didn't want my marriage to end. I didn't want to lose Bill. I was also puzzled and stung to think that Jack would ignore me for so long.

My mother claimed to love her new apartment. On the now-empty hours of my break, I took her shopping for curtains, for a new bedspread, for plants for the patio. The girls rode over on their bicycles after school and my mother offered them cookies and milk and even allowed them to make suggestions for the types of cookies for future afternoons—Maureen and I had been limited to vanilla wafers or graham crackers. Bill brought her a hummingbird feeder and the girls mixed batches of liquid for her so the birds wouldn't be disappointed when they swooped by.

Jonah came by the reference desk and asked me for a drink after work. I told him I had to go right home. He looked unhappy enough for me to feel sorry for him all over again. I think he'd gained even more weight, but at least his nose and eyes weren't running.

Now that the days were getting longer, Bill had both girls out on the public tennis courts and they conspired to get me there, too. I heard the term *doubles* on more than one occasion. Amy retrieved my old racquet for me, but I explained to my daughters as they sandwiched me onto the court that I had poor peripheral vision and even worse hand-eye coordination and they should not expect much from me. They both moaned to let me know that these were not acceptable excuses, that we were about to become a tennis family.

## III

When Jack arrived at the reference desk just as I was about to leave on my break, I saw that things were terribly wrong. There was a pallor under the assertiveness of the tropical tan. Even the starch of his shirt looked less starchy than normal. We drove in the Mazda to the friend's place that looked more gray than ever now with the addition of a thick, charcoal-colored rug under the glass coffee table. He mixed us each a vodka and tonic before he even kissed me. When we finished the drinks, he took my hand and led me to the bed and insisted on undressing me. He'd never before been so passionate, so considerate, or so unhappy.

"She's in the hospital," he said afterward as we lay together. He had his legs thrown over my legs, his head on my shoulder. It was a position Bill often took. I stroked his hair. "Her arm started filling with fluid on the ship the day we arrived in Barbados and there was this feeling of pressure right under her rib cage. She said it felt like indigestion and she decided to ignore it. She wanted the cruise to be happy, you know, but each time we'd reach a port I felt like we were just bumping into some crazy wall. I just wanted to be out of there. It was sup-posed to be a second honeymoon sort of thing."

"You don't have to tell me this," I said. My stomach was already clenching, my throat constricting.

"You've got to understand this. She wanted me to make love to her but I couldn't. There we were lying in this big bed in our stateroom and all we could do together was cry. God, how I cried, but even when I was crying with her I wanted you—I wanted a woman who wasn't dying." He moved his arm so that it rested on my chest. His arm felt like the beam of a building had fallen on me and was crushing me. "Oh, Jesus, it was awful," he said. "She's just so thin now, and her poor little head is like a little baby chicken's body with all this little fluffy hair that's like down on something new, something fresh. And she's rotting inside. Oh, Jesus."

"But you said she was getting better."

"Well, the doctors never say exactly what's going on, but they just did a scan and it's everywhere now. She wants to leave the hospital and spend her last days at home."

"She's dying?"

His hand moved to my breast and rested there. I tightened every muscle in an effort to turn my flesh into some kind of carapace.

"I'm sorry to drop all of this on you. I know this isn't supposed to happen. I know you didn't bargain for this, but then neither did I."

I took his hand away from my breast and brought it to my lips. It was a soft-palmed hand, the fingers narrow and tapering. I kissed the palm of the hand and slid myself away from him. "I have to go."

"I need you," he said. It was almost a whimper. "I told her about us. I'm a confessor. I mean, she's known all along, almost from the start, about you and all of the others. I just haven't been able to resist other women. She was going to leave me years ago, but she didn't. I've always managed to talk her out of it. I'm a good husband in other ways. We have a beautiful house. Financial security. I love our kids. Jesus. It's just this business with women."

"Like me."

"You, yes. And, Jesus, there was a woman on the ship. Beautiful. Red curly hair. A widow. We had a drink while Roxie was sleeping. When she bent over I could see down her dress to her navel. She told me where her room was. I mean, I was giving myself points all during the trip for all the things I wasn't doing, patting myself on the back for being such a good boy."

"I need to go."

"Not yet."

I put on my bra and my panties, my hose, my blouse and skirt, my loafers. I smelled sulphur as he struck a match and lit a cigarette. Then smoke. I smelled him on my hands as I lifted them to push back my hair. My hair would smell of him and of his smoke. The room reeked with our sourness. I had to get away. "I need to go."

"This is agony for me," he said and sat up resting the cigarette on the edge of the nightstand. "Pure agony." His stomach sagged over his groin which beneath its tangle of pubic hair was a ghostly white in contrast to the deep tan above the waist. I wondered if Roxie had gotten tan, too. I fought away a picture of them lying side by side on those ship's lounge chairs, both of them slathered with oil, Roxie in a demure suit that wouldn't subject her tender scars to the equatorial blaze. She'd wear a big hat over her bandana—or her wig. He would hold her hand and be solicitous. He'd suck in his stomach when he stood to walk to the railing where he'd manage to rub against the shoulder of the widow with the red curly hair. Next year he could take another cruise and find more widows with various hair colors who'd whisper their room numbers over margaritas.

I walked the eight blocks to the library facing a southerly wind that promised to bring rain. Maybe it would be one of the last rains of the season. There were only a few trees still in flower. Spring was no longer fresh.

Lately the library had more and more come to resemble a waiting room. A crowd of street people had arrived to establish their positions early, before the rain fell. They slumped in the armchairs, either leafing through magazines or dozing, their day thickly plotted with minutes to be filled. I knew most of their first names. Some were extremely literate and were proud to identify themselves with the library, pleased to be part of an institution that provided both information and shelter.

When I had been a girl in parochial school, I had considered life in a convent. It seemed to be daring to live apart from men. To aspire to a higher love. To reject the mundane. The library had become my convent. I was not celibate, but neither was I monogamous. I was using the tightrope of lust to span the abyss between these poles.

Alice Cortezar, the other reference librarian on then, was in the back room Xeroxing recipes from a new, expensively illustrated Italian cookbook. "Here," she said handing me a sheet of paper, "try this one tonight. Everything I've made from this book is delicious." It was a recipe for fettucini with crab and shrimp in a white wine and cream sauce.

"Bill doesn't eat seafood," I said.

"Oh, dear," she said and gave me a look of true pity, her dark brows coming up, her full lips drawing together. I wished I could store that look, bottle it, preserve it in amber, for the time coming soon when I knew I'd really want it.

Right around six o'clock two police officers strolled in and took away one of our patrons, a sweet-looking young man who had come before noon with one side of his face colored by livid bruises and an abrasion that suggested a skid over cement. He'd taken a chair in the music listening section, put on the headphones, and immediately passed out. He went quietly with only the most modest gestures of protest.

As I was filling in the day's final report forms, I got a call from Jack, who told me he had to see me the next day. He spoke in a whisper and I was sure he was calling from home. "I know I shouldn't have laid all my problems on you," he said, "but you're the only person I can talk to right now. Listen, I'm going nuts. You don't have to give me any advice. I just need someone to hear me."

"You told me already that you're a confessor. I can't absolve you of anything."

"I realize that, and I do feel guilty, you know—I want you to believe that. I'm filled with guilt. It's worse than you know."

"I'm not sure I want to know too much more, Jack."

"I understand," he said. "I'll try to spare you. But I've got to talk to someone."

While I had only considered life in a convent, my sister, Maureen, had actually entered one right after high school at the time when nuns in droves were deserting. She stayed for several years until her small order disbanded because it could no longer support itself. Many of her sister nuns chose to find houses together to try to maintain a semblance of their old life with outside jobs, but at that point Maureen decided to leave for good. She joined an airline as a flight attendant almost as if it were the same sort of thing—a service job helping others on their way to some destination. She stayed on until she gained so much weight that the airline made her leave.

Now she was an obese single woman working in the kitchen of a place that served free lunches to the hungry in downtown Los Angeles. Part of the job involved driving around and begging food from supermarkets and restaurants. Maureen was not only fat now, she could also be terribly smug about her life of good works. She and my mother were in my kitchen sitting on stools beside the counter when I got home. My mother was looking better than she had in months in a new pair of white duck slacks and a pouffy-sleeved green blouse that made her eyes bluer. Maureen had on one of her many muumuus. She had taken lately to wearing a large silver cross that hung between her breasts like a target.

"I make a fantastic spaghetti sauce with ground turkey," Maureen was saying to Bill as he browned hamburger and onion in a large skillet. "Do you have any idea how much damage hooved animals cause on this planet?"

"It's just a matter of taste," he said. "I like the way hamburger tastes." As always, Bill was mild and tolerant.

"Well think of your health at least," she said, giving me the merest nod of acknowledgment.

"I'll give up apples then," he said, "if I have to give up something. They're sure to contain toxic substances at some level."

"Don't you ever cook?" said my mother to me as I put down my bag.

"I cook on weekends." I went to the stove and kissed Bill on the cheek.

"I like to cook," said Bill. "Ellen restores my faith in myself by eating anything I fix."

"I always did the cooking," my mother said. "And I kept house. I could always find the table in my kitchen."

I made a dramatic show of sliding newspapers and books from the table to clear it and dropping them on the floor. "Voilà."

"And even though I cooked every meal, I managed to keep my figure," she said, scowling at Maureen's wide backside.

Maureen acted as if she didn't hear and pointedly pulled a hunk from the loaf of French bread, buttered it, and shoved it into her mouth.

At dinner, Mandy and Amy did their job of diverting us by arguing which was really a better team, the Giants or the A's. Amy was a Giants fan and Mandy rooted for the A's. Each girl, with appalling seriousness, vehemently defended certain perfectly ineffable qualities inherent in each team. The rarified nature of the argument left my mother speechless. The rest of us more or less voted on various points by grunts or nods as we chewed. Maureen had refused Bill's sauce in favor of butter and Parmesan cheese on her spaghetti, having failed to connect the existence of those two food items with hooved animals.

"Mother's praying the rosary, you know," Maureen said as we cleared the dishes. My mother, Bill, and the girls were playing Scrabble in the living room. "I thought she'd given up on the faith."

"I don't know that it means she hasn't," I said. "I know she's stuck in the Sorrowful Mysteries. I'm not sure that's a good sign."

"She still loves our father. I think she's praying for him to come back."

Maureen and I had had this discussion ever since he left us. "I think you want him to come back," I said. "I think you want the circle closed neatly. You want the ideal of the holy family reified."

"That's not fair." She'd brought over a two-liter bottle of red wine for dinner and we'd each had a couple of glasses. Now she sloshed some into a water glass and tilted it back. "I believe in the sanctity of the marriage vow."

"Oh, nonsense," I said. "People say things in a ceremony with a lot of people looking on. It's just some primitive legalistic form. It hasn't anything more to do with life than a rental agreement. If the apartment suits you, you stay. If not, you look for another. You should know. You took a vow too—you were a bride of Christ—and look what happened to you."

"That was different. We were forced to disband."

"Well how do you think Jesus felt?"

"What would you do if Bill did what our father did?" she asked, ignoring my last comment. Her neck was blotched red and the red was spreading to her face.

"Bill's very happy," I said. I poured my own glass, but left it sitting there. "Bill's not like our father."

"But you are, aren't you?" she said. "You're like Dad. I've always suspected you."

"Don't be ridiculous. I love Bill. I love my marriage."

"You've always defended Dad."

"His leaving made me unhappy, too," I said. "I just thought I understood him."

Tears rose in her eyes and began to slide down the sides of her nose. "Oh, Maureen. Don't still be miserable over that. It happened years ago—geologic periods ago."

"I can't help it. I'm lonely and miserable and it's all his fault. If they'd stayed together, I'd have trusted marriage and I wouldn't be the way I am." She let her head fall onto her folded arms and began to cry. Her shoulders heaved. The sounds of the sobs coming from her were terrible, big gulps like hiccups followed by choking.

"Maureen, don't do this." I reached out and touched her shoulder and felt her quiver.

She looked up, her eyes red, her mascara flowing in tiny dark channels down her cheeks. "We're all empty inside. That's what being human means. Only God can fill us up. I eat too much because I've got a hole inside of me that I can't fill up in this world."

"My sister Maureen says that we're all empty and that she eats too much to fill the hole inside her," I said to Jack. We were back in the gray apartment. It was a sudden hot day and the leather couch stuck to the backs of my legs. "Does that make any sense?"

He'd mixed me a vodka with tonic but he was drinking his vodka straight over ice. "It sounds like she's been going to one of those groups where people talk about their feelings."

"I just thought it was interesting."

"Okay, it's interesting. But I've got my own problems. I'm sorry your sister's overweight."

"No, I'm sorry. I know things are rough for you and I wasn't trying to diminish your problems."

"Everybody's sorry." He slammed down the drink and poured another. "You don't have any idea what's going on.

You don't know what my problems are. You have no idea."

"I realize that."

"She came home from the hospital yesterday. We sent the kids to her mother's so we could be alone. She said she wanted to talk. Do you know what she wanted to talk about?"

I didn't say anything. I could think of several topics Roxie might have chosen. Jack tried to get the glass up to his lips, but his hand began to tremble. The glass slipped from his fingers. His eyes followed its descent with as much horror as if it had been a bomb. When it struck the floor and shattered, he looked truly puzzled, as if he couldn't remember how the pieces of glass, the cubes of ice, the liquid had gotten there.

I went to the kitchen for some paper towels. He followed me, stopped me at the sink, and turned me around, holding my arm so that I had to face him. "She wanted me to help her die," he said. "Roxie had some idea that I could help her die."

"What do you mean?" There was a sudden buzzing inside my skull as if he'd touched a switch. His voice seemed to be coming from a distant planet and yet I could smell his breath, the onions he'd had for lunch before the vodka.

"I wasn't sure. I don't think she was sure. She talked about me getting a gun for her—a pistol—or maybe a shotgun. She talked about how sometimes with a pistol you could miss, even if you held it in your mouth—miss and then be a vegetable but not dead. She talked about poison. I told her that I couldn't even listen to her talk this way, that I hoped she wasn't really serious. I begged her not to ask me to help her."

I held onto the counter as he tightened his grip. His

right knee, the bad one, buckled, and he tilted like a toy. Using my arm, he pulled himself up. "She said that if I loved her, I'd put a pillow over her face. 'I love you, Roxie,' I told her, 'I'll be here for you. I'll try to see that you don't have any pain, but I can't help you die.'" His fingers bit into my arm. He licked his lips.

His eyes were having a hard time focusing, shifting from the memory inside his head to me standing in front of him. A twitch on the left side of his face followed each shift. "She turned away from me and looked at the wallpaper. It's a print paper with roses all over the wall. Big fucking cabbage roses. We put the paper up together when we first moved into the house. She stared at the damn roses and wouldn't look at me anymore, as if I wasn't worth looking at. She just stared—all slumped over, and I knew I'd failed her again."

"Don't Jack," I whispered. "Don't tell me any more."

"Shut up," he said. His hand was a tourniquet on my arm. "I mean I've just failed her over and over and over. Finally, minutes later, she said, 'It's okay, Jack.' The way she said it made my heart sink. 'It's okay,' she said, dismissing me, you know, like one of the kids in her class who couldn't ever get things right. 'You do what you have to, Jack.'"

"I don't want to be here," I said. I was sweating but beneath the sweat my skin was icy.

"I understand, Ellen. But I need company now. I don't want to be alone now."

"Go back to her Jack. Go back to Roxie."

"I can't. Not now. She won't have me now. I need to be with someone. You're in this, too."

"No." I shook my head and tore away from him and went to the living room and knelt by the broken glass.

Gingerly, I began picking up the bright slivers, the shards. "No. I'm on the outside, Jack. I'm not in that part of your life, Jack. Did you forget that?"

"She knows about you. You're involved."

"If it hadn't been me it would have been someone else, and you know it." I had the pieces of glass resting in the palm of my hand. I got up and went to the wastebasket but he grabbed my wrist.

"Do you know what she's doing at this very moment?" he asked, holding my wrist so I couldn't drop the glass. I swayed and shook my head. "She asked me to leave the house. She's been saving pills. All this time in the hospital, they've been bringing her two pills, she only takes one and saves the other."

"Let me go." I hadn't meant to scream but I heard my voice echo back from the hard gray walls. I twisted away and the glass spun from my hand. His face looking into mine was fierce. Fierce and without recognition. His odd, almost pupilless eyes swam in their whites. His tan was like a filthy mask. He seemed to grow taller, become attentuated, and in an odd way almost purified by his rage. I ran out into the hall and down the steps onto the sidewalk where the sudden May sunlight wiped out the world.

I forgot that I had a car. When I arrived at my mother's apartment, I was shivering and my teeth were chattering. She let me in without a word and I fell onto her couch. "I'm sick," I said. "You have to take care of me."

"What do you mean, you're sick?" She frowned and stayed by the door, leaving it open as if there was a chance that I'd need to bolt as quickly as I'd come in.

"I think I have some kind of flu. I just want to rest."

"You have a home, you know. Why aren't you there?"

"I'm shivering, Mother. Let me stay here."

She stayed by the door keeping her distance from me. "I just put fresh sheets on my bed. Go on in there."

Her eyes had gone to my skirt. "You're bleeding," she said.

I looked down and saw that there was a cut in the palm of my hand. Streaks of blood smeared across my skirt. "It's just a little cut," I said. "Broken glass."

I stayed in her bed sliding in and out of sleep. Perhaps I really did have a flu. From time to time outside of the door I heard voices. Bill came in and sat by me, and then a doctor, a friend he played tennis with, arrived to examine me. The girls whispered to me and left and came back with flowers they'd picked. My father came in and held my hand, which someone had bandaged. My mother was sitting beside me when I opened my eyes the next time. Then I slept.

My mother had a cup of tea on a tray on the bedside table. I pulled myself up and let her arrange pillows so I could sit. Her face looked different. There was an odd lopsided smile now. A single lamp on the nightstand lit the room. Beyond the curtains, a street light created a false moon. I was a little girl again. I'd returned home after a long time. I could remember another life in between then and now but it seemed blurred like a scene glimpsed through the window of a racing train.

"Your father and I are having lunch together tomorrow," she said, bending over me with the tray.

"Oh, Mother," I said. I must have wailed or moaned the words, because she stood up and gave me a disturbed, frightened look. "Mother, don't get led into all of that stuff again. He's not going to change. Don't get your hopes up," I said.

She continued to stand there with the tray in her hand but her face relaxed, and the smile—lopsided and guileless, amazingly guileless—returned. "I know that. I'm not expecting miracles. It will just be nice to talk to him again after all these years. We're not married anymore."

"As long as you understand that," I said. I let her place the tray on my lap. The tea was strong and bitter. There was a piece of toast too and I ate that with her standing beside the bed watching my every bite.

"Do you want me to roll the television in here and we could watch together?" she asked when I'd finished.

"No. I think I'll rest again." I was as exhausted from eating as if I'd climbed a mountain. She left the door slightly open and I heard the sound of television voices and then the theme of the late news show and then voices again and finally the weather for the next day, then quiet. I must have slept again but I woke to the sound of my mother's voice—chanting, rhythmic, rising, and falling—and I recognized the words. She was saying the rosary.

"Are you still on the Sorrowful Mysteries?" I asked when she came in later.

"Yes," she said, "but I see the possibility of moving on to the Joyful now."

"And from there to the Glorious?"

"I don't believe in rushing things," she said and closed the door.

My mother is a better person than I had believed. She has allowed my father to make peace with her. They've had lunch twice now, and although I know they will never be together again, they appear to have rediscovered something in the other that had been mislaid. Some kinds of change, it seems, are possible after all.

On the morning I went back to work, I read the obituary for Roxanne Muller Duggan. She was forty-one years old. There would be no service. Donations could be made in her memory to the Walnut Grove Science Education Program.

That same morning, I talked to Ben Michaelson and we agreed to exchange shifts so that he could take classes in the afternoon. I would lunch from noon to one and be home when Bill returned. Then I went to Section 635—Gardening—and gathered a stack of books for my book sack.

On my lunch break I took a walk along the creek in a nearby park. It was one of those sun-choked late-May days, somnolent with a sense of spring fulfilled, that grants its own form of grace. I am sure that it had never occurred to Bill that I might have another life, and I have decided that he must not find out. I hope for the best. We don't need to know everything.

# Solstice

IT WAS THE DAY the Murphy's Shetland pony Fiesta
broke down Tilly Worth's garden fence and ate all the
Kentucky Wonders as well as the marijuana plants Tilly
grew to supplement her Social Security, the day Walt
Tarver found two women making love in his barn, and
the day the Polonius brothers' compost pile caught fire
and the fire truck broke an axle on the road up to put it
out. It was the loveliest day of the year, the longest
sweetest day, the day when summer is still a new idea,
and it was the day Rita Tooley wound up with two lovers
and couldn't make up her mind.

Neither of the men was perfect. But Rita wasn't the sort
to mind. She bought her clothes in the flea market, and she
fastened her ideas together with the happy glue of coinci-
dence. She liked cups with chips, and men with flaws.
Rita was beautiful but no beauty. She was small and a bit
heavy. Her hair was abundant but wild, and her smile
wide but off center. Her eyes were innocent of meaness
and she cooked like an angel.

On solstice morning Rita woke in her bed with Joe
beside her. She always woke with the first light and often
envied Joe's ability to sleep until roused. But this morning
she envied no one. A mockingbird had been rehearsing
its arias for hours, and beside her Joe snored gently, breaking his own rhythms with little grunts and murmurs. She
moved closer to him and put her face barely an inch from
his and let his breath flow onto it. Joe was the only man

she had ever slept with whose breath was sweet in the morning.

It would be a perfect day. She would serve breakfast in her little cafe downstairs to the tourists who came through town on their way to the ocean and then she would serve lunch to others who were late going or early returning and then she would close and let those who wanted dinner go to one of the big places farther along. Then she would pack a basket and she and Joe would drive to a ridge and drink wine and eat cold chicken and salmon and fresh bread and summer tomatoes and watch the last light dissolve into the ocean.

This, however, was not to be.

For Beck was on his way, even at that moment, in the old silver Mercedes he'd won in a card game the day before in Reno. Beck had been away at a place with the resortlike name of Deer Lodge. It had been a mix-up, he'd said all along, a mix-up having something to do with a transportation problem and with finding that the truck he was driving had been filled with freezers and televisions acquired in irregular ways. And because he was Beck, he believed his own story and was on his way back to Rita, who he knew would believe it, too. He hadn't called her or written her in the last year because Rita wasn't the sort of person you called or wrote if things weren't perfectly fine. With Rita you needed a face-to-face. After this face-to-face he was sure things would be right once more.

"Would you like bacon or sausage with your eggs?" Rita asked Walt Tarver, though she knew that he always

58

took sausage. She also knew that he always wanted to order and never tolerated assumptions being made on his behalf. He owned almost everything in the area and he wasn't one of those to whom Rita could ask, "The regular this morning?" As she wrote down Walt's order, she looked up and smiled good-bye to Joe, who was leaving the kitchen with his lunch bag and Thermos for another day of nailing and sawing on a fancy house that some city people were building on the old Bernard place.

Then, not a minute later, she got to smile at Joe again as he came back in. "Can I use your car today?" he asked, flashing his two rows of peerless human porcelain. "I'm out of gas and too late to get some."

"Yes, but be sure you leave me your keys."

"You got it," he said and bent to kiss her, letting her smell his mint toothpaste and lime shaving cream, the flowery soap and strawberry shampoo and a bit of Joe musk beneath it all—so much scent that she became dizzy with pleasure and wild with longing for him to return so she could bury her face in the presence of him.

And Beck was on his way, driving fast and eating an early apple he'd borrowed from a tree on the roadside. He was driving fast, but not so fast that he didn't notice, as he headed down the grade into the little valley called Tarver's Crossing that his own 1957 Volkswagen was coming up toward him. It was the car he'd been given by a friend in lieu of a small debt, the car he'd loaned to Rita over a year ago when her car threw a rod. And there it was, passing him on its way up as he was on the way down, driven not by Rita but by someone entirely different —driven by a man.

I wonder who that son-of-a-bitch is, Beck asked himself without rancor as he tossed the apple core out of the window—and for the first time it occurred to him that in the space of a year things might have changed. This idea disturbed him so much that when he got to town he decided to take time just to drive by the Mermaid Cafe— Rita's place—and then to drive around all six square blocks of Tarver's Crossing to satisfy himself that nothing had gone on without his knowledge.

After completing this loop to his satisfaction, he stopped in at the Manhood Tavern for a visit with Charlie Manhood —and a beer, though he normally didn't drink before evening.

"Beck, you're in town!" Charlie said.

"Give me something on tap," Beck said. "I see that things have stayed the same—more or less." And he raised the glass of beer that Charlie slid his way, toasting the morning regulars at the other end—the Polonius brothers and a Basque whose name Beck could never remember. All three, stiffened by age, seemed more like taxidermic exhibits than men, but they managed to raise their glasses, which glinted in the dusty shafts of morning light.

"More or less," Charlie said. Like most barkeepers, he was laconic.

"It looks about the same."

"On vacation, were you?" Charlie asked.

"You could say that," Beck said.

"You been by the Mermaid yet?"

"Not yet. How's Rita?"

"About the same," Charlie said and looked down at the section of bar he was polishing as if some nick in the finish might suddenly yawn into a gulf.

When Rita looked up from the coffee maker to see Beck standing in the doorway, framed there, neither in nor out, her body gave a jolt as if it were on the receiving end of an electrical current. Her knees almost buckled beneath her, and she began vibrating like a tuning fork.

Beck took a step forward and removed himself from the tentative hold of her doorway. "Turned to stone, are you," he said, "by the sight of me?"

"I can't move," she answered, in a whisper—which really wasn't necessary since the breakfast crowd had gone and there was no one in the place. She whispered because she doubted that she could take a step forward to where he stood with his sideways smile showing a bit of the gold incisor, his bottle green eyes looking at her and into her, and his voice both rough and tender as the bark on a tree.

"I haven't touched anyone in over a year," he said, "and I don't know if I can touch you now. Help me, will you?"

"Beck," she said and managed to take a step forward and stretch out her hand. "Oh, Beck . . ."

"Rita," he said and took another step, and another, and reached out his hand and almost, but not quite, touched hers, almost but not quite, so that the spark of need could jump the gap from finger to finger.

They were in each other's arms in a second and their embrace was long. When finally they pulled apart for a breath of air, Rita placed the *Closed* sign in the window and went into the kitchen to tell Cherry Vivaldi, the college girl who helped out in the summer, that she was free for the day.

An hour or so later, Beck lay on Rita's bed like a man who had come through a desert and finally had a chance to drink deep. Rita lay beside him, her hair wet with sweat and sticking to his chest, her heart finally slowing down.

He slept. She slept. And when he woke he noticed clothes he had never seen in her closet, and a pair of boxer shorts on the floor. He wore Jockeys.

When Rita woke she remembered that she hadn't heard from Beck for more than a year and that she had let him just walk over her threshold as if the entire path of the earth in its orbit had been pulled in like a belt to let him account for no more than a normal absence from her. And she also saw the pair of boxer shorts on the floor by the dresser, and the pair of Jockeys on the floor on the rug by the bed, and she realized that she had a problem.

Beck cleared his throat.

Rita sat up in bed and pulled the sheet up to cover her breasts.

"Who?" said Beck.

"Joe—the carpenter."

"He's just a kid. You've got to be joking."

"He's legal and he's a keeper."

"He was driving my car!"

"His truck was out of gas." She got out of bed and, taking the sheet with her, went to the closet and looked for something to wear.

Beck leaned over and found his Jockeys. He turned his back to her when he put them on. Then, with his loins girded in baggy cotton knit, he faced her. "I love you, Rita."

"I love you, too," she whispered, still holding the sheet. "There was never any question of that."

At this very moment the siren, which Charlie Manhood had mounted on the roof of his tavern, sounded, announcing a fire. The next moment Rita's phone rang. It was Charlie saying that the VFD was a man shy on the fire truck and wondering if Beck would like to resume his position as volunteer.

"We'll talk about this later," Beck said to Rita and slipped into his jeans.

At this point things got a bit complicated and even those watching intently might have missed something.

As the fire truck on its way to put out the fire at the Polonius place ascended the narrow hillside road, Walt Tarver was descending the same road in his pickup with the two women he had discovered in his barn. They had been making love on the seat of a 1942 Reo truck that once belonged to his dead father, and he was taking them at gunpoint to the sheriff. They had been naked and avid, and their absorption in their passion made it possible for him to come upon them with a loaded .45—which he continued to hold on them while they dressed. Walt's outrage grew from the fact that this particular trespass not only violated the hallowed law of private property but also what he believed to be a law of nature. He saw the use of the truck seat as adding insult to injury by profaning the memory of his father.

Now it isn't easy to drive a stick-shift truck over a rocky road while holding a loaded gun on people. Even Walt, in his fury, had sense enough to know that if the gun went off and a bullet chanced to hit one of the women, he would not be without legal problems. So things were not in perfect control when Tom Scarlatti, at the wheel of the fire truck, rounded a bend and found Walt bearing down on him, either unable or unwilling to give way.

Tom made an effort to avoid collision and timing seemed to favor him. He was approaching the steep driveway up to the Polonius place and was about to turn on to it. Unfortunately, just at that moment, Joe, driving Beck's Volkswagen, was rushing down the driveway to head off the fire department, to spare them the trip up the tortuous road, with the information that the fire, a spontaneous combustion in a compost pile, was under control. He had seen it from where he was working on the ridge above, driven down, and doused it with a garden hose.

To avoid another collision, Tom swerved again and wound up with his right front tire in a ditch and a broken axle. Walt slammed on his brakes, but they failed to grip the loose gravel of the road and the right front of his pickup struck the rear of the stalled fire truck, which sent the pickup over the edge of the road and down through Murphy's orchard and through the fence that had prevented Fiesta the Shetland pony from nibbling at the green world beyond the tired brown earth of her yard. Walt managed to hold onto both the gun and the steering wheel during this and so was able to march his captives, one of whom had a slight concussion from contact with the windshield, back up the hill.

The blow from Walt's pickup sent Beck, who had been riding on the rear of the fire truck, flying off to sprawl in the dirt, a vantage point from which he got to watch Joe climb out of the Volkswagen and approach him. Beck had no way of knowing that Joe had only seen a body leave the pump truck and land on the ground, and that Joe had no idea who the owner of that body was.

"Don't touch me, you son-of-a-bitch," Beck said as Joe, concern wrinkling his young smooth brow, bent over him.

"Beck?" Joe said, and then, "Beck! What are you doing here?"

Rita, meanwhile, was growing frantic with anxiety, remorse, and misgiving. Months ago she had worn herself out with guilt over having let things with Joe get started, but at the time it had seemed the only thing to do.

Now she loved him. But now Beck was here, and she loved him, too. After she watched Beck run down to the firehouse, she slowly began to get dressed, but that didn't seem like the right thing to do so she took off her clothes and flung herself naked on the bed and cried. Then she got up and dressed again.

She took the *I Ching* and the coins from the shelf by her bed. Then she put them back. She took off her clothes again and crawled into bed and pulled the sheet over her face to lie still as a corpse and wonder what life would be like if she had to give up either man. She wondered if this were some ultimate test that she might fail and, in failing, be stripped forever of her right to love.

After an hour or so under the sheet, she got up and dressed again. She wasn't good at passive anguish so she went down into the kitchen and began to do things.

She took out flour and yeast and soon there was dough rising. She went to her garden and picked tomatoes and cucumbers and green and red peppers, and onions, and fresh basil, dill, tarragon, sage, and rosemary. She kneaded herbs into the dough. She took out several chickens from the refrigerator and rubbed them with herbs and garlic and poured wine and olive oil over them. She brought out a salmon and stuffed it with breadcrumbs and garlic and herbs. She pulled down bottles of wine and placed them in a wash tub and covered them with ice. And she hummed as she did this. Hums that became incantations. She cried sometimes and sometimes she smiled. It was hot in the kitchen and she opened all the doors and windows and set up fans to keep the breezes flowing.

"Don't touch me!" Beck said again. Then he groaned as the pain reached him. His leg was twisted behind him and he straightened it very slowly. Next he moved his arms, one at a time. He felt as if he needed oil in every joint.

"Beck," Joe said again.

"Can't you think of anything else to say?" Beck said.

"No."

"Do you want to fight?"

"No," Joe said. "I'm a coward."

"I can't fight you, anyway, you son-of-a-bitch," Beck said, "because I've just had the piss knocked out of me. But you deserve something. You moved in on my woman."

"You never even wrote to her. She used to cry about it all the time. I had to hold her in my arms while she cried."

"Oh, hell!" Beck said and lost consciousness.

Which spared him the pain of having to watch the two women, one tall and beautiful with blood streaming from her forehead, the other almost a dwarf, crest the hill with Walt Tarver holding a gun on them and watch Walt push them into Beck's own Volkswagen, the tall one first into the backseat where she collapsed and the short one, stoic, in the front.

"Hey, " Joe yelled, "you can't take that car!"

"I'm making a citizen's arrest," Walt said, and with that he started the tiny engine and drove down the hill to the town that bore the name of his father, a man who had earned the right to name a town by stripping all the trees from all the hills for miles around and turning them into lumber.

Just as Walt disapppeared around the bend, the Polonius brothers came down their driveway in their truck. Two hunting dogs, ancient as their owners, sat in the back and sniffed the wind without much interest, merely paying homage to a memory of things wild. The Polonius brothers were on their way to the Manhood Tavern for their afternoon beer. It took very little to persuade them, the promise of a couple of free drinks each, to get them to take the unconscious Beck and the rest of the fire crew down with them. Joe said he would walk, for he needed time to think.

As the truck bounced over the rocks and through the potholes, Beck dreamed. He dreamed that he went down some stairs into a cellar where a card game was going on. At first he thought the game was poker, but then it seemed that it was some more complicated game where bets were made not on the cards but on other factors that Beck didn't understand. One man, a thin consumptive guy, was betting everything on his hand. He even took off his watch and shoes and put them on the table. Yet he had a terrible hand. It was nuts to bet on that hand. But then, after he bet, the guy's cards changed. Beck witnessed this himself because he was standing right behind the guy looking down. The little red and black spots merged together and grew and spread, and suddenly the guy was holding a royal flush. Beck began to breath heavily. He knew he had money in his pocket, but just as he was trying to get into the game, Tom Scarlatti lifted him up in his strong arms and Beck felt himself being carried into the Manhood Tavern and placed on a pool table in the back room.

As Beck dreamed, Joe walked. Thought, Joe knew, was not his long suit. He felt guilty and vulnerable. He had known that Beck loved Rita, that Rita loved Beck, but he had fallen in love with Rita, too. He had loved her from the first time he worked for her building the new counters in her kitchen and making the big maple cutting board that ran the length of the room, measuring it and putting it together, smelling the smells of new bread and fresh-cut wood marry in the warm bright room where Rita cooked while he worked. He had known then that Beck was in jail, and he understood that something— shame or fear—kept Beck from writing Rita, but when she'd cried, and he'd held her, had felt her tangled hair under his chin, her sobbing head against his chest, he knew he didn't care. In fact, he hoped the authorities would find more freezers and televisions or whatever it was that had gotten Beck in trouble and keep him there even longer.

He wanted to do the honorable thing, but he wasn't sure what that was. He could go away. Instead of going back to town when he got down to the main road, he could stick out his thumb and be somewhere else in no time. Rita would understand, and tears would come to her eyes whenever she thought of him.

As he turned a bend and arrived at the main road, Joe was joined by an unsteady pony, a pony who looked him in the eye and appeared to be waiting for him. The pony had a far-off gaze like that of statues in church, and yet

the pony seemed to be staring directly into Joe's eyes—
and even further than that. Joe had no idea what this pony
was seeing and it made him uneasy. He tried to ignore the
pony but the pony refused to ignore him. It placed itself
in his path. Then it occurred to Joe that the pony wanted
him to get on and ride it, which struck him as pretty silly
since it was a small animal and he was a large man. There
was something so implacable in the pony's look, however, that he got on and, with his feet dragging the
ground, he allowed himself to be carried to the door of
the Manhood Tavern.

Inside the tavern a party seemed to be getting started.
The Polonius brothers were sipping the drinks they'd
been promised and had ordered Charlie's best brandy.
The Basque who was the caretaker at Murphy's was trying to find out why Tarver's truck had wound up in
Fiesta's pen, and trying to figure out where the pony was.
Tilly Worth had arrived. She had chased Fiesta out of her
garden and had gone to complain about it to the Basque
who wasn't there. Tilly knew the habits of the Basque
and decided to confront him here—where he drank. Tom
Scarlatti, the VFD's paramedic, had examined Beck's ankle
and decided along with Beck that it was a sprain, and that
he should just keep his weight off it when he walked.

Beck, disconsolate over matters far worse than a
sprained ankle, was drinking whiskey with a beer chaser.
The two women who had been taken at gunpoint arrived
after being admonished and released by the sheriff. The
small woman introduced herself as Bright Hawk, and was
recognized as a legendary lady wrestler. Her friend—tall
and beautiful, whose name was never announced—allowed
Tom to put a bandage on her forehead. And the crew of

the Tarver's Crossing VFD, who had sweated under their slickers on a mission to save a compost pile, looked on as they sipped their beers.

Joe took a seat at the end of the bar opposite Beck and ordered a beer with a whiskey chaser. He was aware that everyone in the room had surmised what the situation was between himself and Beck.

One of the Polonius brothers elbowed the other and they both grinned at the same time. They weren't twins, but they were so alike and had lived together so long that no one was sure who was who anymore. Together they looked from Joe to Beck, and then from Beck to Joe. After this appraisal, they conferred and when they looked up again their grins were even wider.

"Hey, Charlie, bring Joe the dice!" said Milt—or was it Mack?

"Hey, Beck, you and the kid roll the dice. Take care of it that way," said the other.

"It seems like Rita ought to have a word in this," said Joe as Beck scowled.

In Rita's kitchen, her long counter bravely upheld the labors of the afternoon. It stood heaped with loaves of bread, with succulent chickens, with tender salmon, with piles of vegetables reeling under olive oil and vinegar and garlic. Wet with perspiration, head in hands, shoulders shaking with the force of her weeping, Rita sat beside these offerings.

This is the sight that Cherry Vivaldi, passing on her way down to meet her lover Tom Scarlatti at the Manhood Tavern, saw when she looked in after smelling the odors of all of that wonderful food.

"Rita!" she said. "I thought you'd closed."

"Oh, Cherry," Rita wailed, looking up. "I'm so miserable."

"What's wrong?" Cherry asked and knelt beside Rita, taking her hand and holding it.

"It's about love," sobbed Rita. "Do you think love ever really makes anyone happy?"

"Oh," said Cherry. She and Tom had just fallen in love and she wasn't the right person to ask, but she was willing to consider this. "I don't know," she said finally, "but it makes them glad."

"Oh, Cherry," sobbed Rita and threw her arms around the young woman's shoulders. "I love them both."

Cherry, who had been present when Beck arrived, knew what Rita was talking about. "That's a problem." She squeezed Rita's hand to show her deepest sympathy. "But things may just work out." Cherry was a born optimist. She was also curious. "What are you going to do with all this food?"

"I don't know," Rita said. "I just had this urge to cook."

"We could have a picnic. That should cheer you up. Tom and I were going to the reservoir to swim. We could invite people. Why don't you wash up and come with us? It would be better than sitting here feeling terrible."

"I don't want to," Rita said. "Just take the food."

"No," said Cherry. "No you, no picnic."

That's why, a little later Cherry led Rita into the Manhood Tavern to count heads for the picnic. Before this could happen, however, Rita had to face both Beck and Joe, who sat at the bar as if they were waiting for her. They both turned when the door opened, and both of them watched her walk into the center of the room. She was pale and her dark eyes looked like two coals in a snowbank.

Everyone stopped talking and waited.

"I've made some mistakes in my life," Rita said, acknowledging the fact that a public testimony was expected. Her voice had such a delicate quaver to it that almost everyone thought she would falter and not go on, but she continued. People leaned forward straining to hear. "But not in love," she said, and her voice grew stronger. "I fell in love with two men and I don't want to give up either of them." She paused and looked straight ahead, as if afraid to turn in either's direction for fear she might be swayed. "That's all there is to it. I want them both. I can love them both."

No one said anything for a long time. One of the Polonius brothers' dogs howled outside, but everyone acted as if the dog was howling on Mars. Beck stared into his glass, Joe at the lamp over Rita's head. Then, when they finally spoke, they both did it together.

"Okay," said Beck.

"Sure," said Joe.

The Polonius brothers were the first to begin clapping. But everyone else joined in.

"You guys could roll for the evenings, if you'll pardon the expression," said Charlie and he lifted the leather cup with the poker dice.

"Okay," said Beck.

"Sure," said Joe.

The Polonius brothers used their truck to bring the food up to the reservoir. Everyone else walked—even Beck, who limped but wouldn't let anyone help him. When they reached the pool in the woods, they found it to be the color of the sky and streaked with the reds and pinks of sunset.

They lost no time in shedding their clothes. No one was coy. The Basque tried to keep on his beret, but when he dove in it came off and floated away and he didn't seem to notice. Bright Hawk and her friend walked in holding hands and then they did the backstroke together in such marvelous synchronization that Charlie Manhood thought of Esther Williams and almost cried. Tilly Worth, who was just getting over being furious with Fiesta, tiptoed to the water's edge and splashed herself before wading in, a gesture so demure and deliberate that both of the Polonius brothers got their first erections in fifteen years. The men of the VFD ran in, drill style, and splashed and snorted and then chose sides in order to chicken fight. Cherry and Tom swam off together to the far side to kiss and whisper and promise that they'd never be foolish. And Rita held Beck's hand on one side and Joe's on the other and the three waded out and allowed themselves to be suspended by the water. The sunset lasted and lasted and the light became more and more like molten silver. When they finally came out of the pool, they found themselves shining.

# Taking Fire

THE TOW TRUCK backed the dark green Chevrolet into a space and it became one of a line of cars on the back lot behind the Gulf Service Station, but everybody knew it wasn't just an ordinary car anymore. Even the almost-new 1957 Ford Fairlane with the caved-in roof a few cars down, a Ford that had taken the life of Red Landry on the famous Dead Man's Curve on Military Road only a week before, wasn't in the running.

Meat Daigle, who owned the Gulf Station, shooed people away. He knew the car was special but he didn't know how to handle it yet, so he placed his bulk between the car and those of us looking on, and that seemed to be barrier enough.

As we were moving away, I saw my father drive by on his way home to lunch and I ducked behind a gas pump. Watching a tow truck bring in the car in which two people had just that morning been found dead after having been missing for more than five days wasn't the sort of entertainment that he would approve of for his seventeen-year-old daughter. I ducked behind a pump even though I didn't think he'd see me. He always drove with his eyes straight ahead on the road, expecting the worst. As soon as he was gone, Lorraine, Tom, and I got into Tom's mother's new Buick Roadmaster and drove to the Dairy Freeze. Nobody talked. Lorraine and I got cones but threw them away when they started to melt because we couldn't eat them.

"I'm going to be sick," Lorraine said. "I can't believe

we just did that—went there." She looked like she might
actually throw up. Her plump, olive-skinned face had an
odd gray cast. Her eyes looked glazed. Lorraine was very
emotional. She even wept over the stuffed animals that
cluttered her bed. She had been my neighbor for years
and there was a bond of time between us, but mostly she
made me impatient.

"I would have gone over to see the inside of the car if
Meat hadn't been there," Tom said. "Just to see."

"Just to see what? They're gone," I said.

"Just to see," Tom said. Then he shrugged and backed
up the Buick and threw his paper cup half full of milk
shake out of the window.

"What's that stuff called again, Patsy?" Lorraine asked
me, frowning. Lorraine's mind seemed not to have been
intended to store facts. "The stuff that killed them."

"Carbon monoxide," I said. "We studied it in chemistry. Remember?"

"I guess I was absent that day," Lorraine said. "Take me
home. I have to baby-sit this afternoon."

With Lorraine gone, Tom and I drove out to Old Landing, a clearing in the woods on the deeper part of the
river where some pilings from an ancient pier jutted out
of the water. If you didn't know the history, that boats
came across the lake and up the river from New Orleans
and unloaded here once, you'd probably think what was
left of the pilings were just big cypress knees. Old Landing was the local make-out place. During the day black
people came here to fish, but at night cars drove up and
turned off their lights and parked under the low-hanging
branches of oak trees. Today the place was deserted.

We parked. Neither of us could think of anything to

say. Tom got out and I followed him. He picked up a stick and threw it into the water and three turtles scuttled off a log and swam away. The October sun was low—just behind the trees and their shadows were long on the murky water.

"It's like a bad, a really bad, joke," Tom said finally. "People were laughing about it, but nobody felt good."

"It's like the worst joke," I said. "To be found out like that. He had four little children over in Bethel, and they and his wife and her mother were at a prayer service when it happened."

"They went to the carnival. She was eating cotton candy. The Ferris wheel broke and they got stuck at the top for a half an hour."

"How do you know that?"

"Somebody at the gas station saw them there."

"So they were at the carnival before they went to park?"

"Yeah," Tom said and laughed, a laugh that stopped short. He bent and picked up another stick and threw it in the water. It was a small stick and the splash wasn't much.

"Well, if they'd come here to Old Landing, it wouldn't have taken five days to find them. They'd have been found in about half an hour. Everybody comes here." I picked up a stick and threw it in the water, too. I couldn't think of anything else to do then.

"Jesus," Tom said. He walked back to the car. I followed him, got in, and turned on the radio. The Everly brothers were singing "Wake Up Little Susie." I turned it off.

Tom didn't get in but stood by the car looking around. Maybe he was fixing in his mind the location of each tree and each rut in the road and each piece of ground where the grasses had been flattened by car tires. I was. "I think I'll check the oil," he said.

"You just checked it a few days ago."

"I promised my mother I'd check the oil if I used the car," he said.

When he got back in the car, I moved over next to him and put my hand on his thigh. I wanted to touch him. I always wanted to touch him. I couldn't keep my hands off him. I'd never been like that with a boy before. I'd always been able to be the cool one, the one to turn on the ice, but Tom made me a little nuts.

I couldn't explain it to myself. I was older than he was. I was a senior and he was only a junior. He wasn't that handsome. He had sandy hair that was soft and couldn't even stand up as a crew cut. He wore glasses, but when he took them off to kiss me, I couldn't stop looking at his soft gray unfocused eyes. Somehow knowing he couldn't really see me up so close made him seem beautifully flawed and gave me a sense of power. He turned to me and slid his hand up under my shirt and started to unhook my brassiere. I reached up and took off his glasses for him. Taking off Tom's glasses was like undressing him. We tried to kiss but both of our mouths were dry as dust.

"Leroy Odum says that the bodies were melted together," my brother Davis said that night at dinner. He had been mixing up his green peas and mashed potatoes, swirling them with his fork. "The sun just cooked them in that car as if they'd been in a pot in the oven. They were birthday naked and their clothes were in a heap on the front seat."

"This is not a topic for dinner conversation," my father said. "Or conversation anywhere." He had a piece of meat halfway to his mouth but put the fork down on his plate.

"The whole event is just better forgotten," my mother

said after she'd swallowed. Her face was puffy and damp. She always seemed to be perspiring—even when it was cold. "It's just unspeakable."

"I knew who he was," Davis continued. He was thirteen and still felt that it was worthwhile to try to talk to our parents. "He drove the bulldozer over at the pine oil factory. She was a waitress at Carmichael's."

"I think everyone is familiar with this information," my father said. "I think I have heard this repeated at least fifty times today." My father was a pharmacist and generally heard everything. There had once been a soda fountain in his drugstore which had attracted people. When he took out the fountain to get more shelf space and replaced it with a Coke machine, people still came and stood around talking, with bottles of Coke in their hands.

Even though he heard it all there behind the prescription counter, my father never repeated anything. He felt that the drugstore was a hallowed place and he, like doctors and lawyers, had a sacred duty to keep all the gossip that he received within those walls confidential. People trusted him, it's true, but I always thought this notion of his made him a pretty boring person.

"It makes you wonder, though..." my mother said and squinted across the room as though looking for something in the china cabinet there.

"They were trashy people," my father said. "Trashy people do trashy things."

"They died for love," Lorraine said.

"They died because of love," I said. "It's different." Lorraine and Tom and I were driving around after school in my father's Studebaker, a ridiculous car, that my father had bought several years ago because he thought it was what the cars of the future would look like and, by buying it as soon as it came out, he would be recognized as a visionary during his lifetime. We had just driven by the hill of pine knots beside the pine oil factory. An old straw-hatted man was driving the bulldozer today. Several other cars were also driving by the pine oil factory, which was unusual. Hardly any traffic ever went along this pothole-pitted back street. I figured if we saw any of the same cars passing by our next stop, Carmichael's, we'd know that we were part of some sort of sorry pilgrimage.

There was a small crowd at Carmichael's, a narrow place between the hardware and a florist, more than you'd expect at 3:30 on a Friday afternoon. People our age didn't go to Carmichael's. It didn't have a jukebox, just a radio tuned to a station that played country music alternating with farm bulletins. Afternoons were for the pie-and-coffee set, the local businessmen, the farmers who came into town for the day, and women who'd spent a taxing afternoon at the Ben Franklin or Shultz's Dry Goods.

"This was her dress," I heard one of the waitresses— a fat woman with tight blue sausage curls and small close-set eyes—say to a woman in a red flowered house coat. "She left it on this peg here in the hall and changed into a regular dress in the ladies' room. She was wearing a little rabbit-fur jacket she'd just gotten, and I think he probably helped her pay for it, because how else . . . ?"

"However else . . . ?" the woman in red echoed as if there was really no question about that sort of thing. She looked at the dress but stood back from it as if it might be carrying some disease the way that blankets the white men gave to the Indians carried smallpox germs.

"This was her dress, Ruth," the woman in red said to

another woman who came up to her. I slid along behind them and went to the ladies' room and waited inside next to the door until they'd gone. Then I came out and passed the dress, brushing against it, letting it touch my face. It was a pink cotton dress with a white collar and cuffs. I closed my eyes for a second, feeling it against my cheek. It smelled of sweat and Evening in Paris dusting powder. I knew about Evening in Paris. My father sold it. My mother preferred Coty's.

"They had the radio tuned to 'Randy's Record Shop.'" Tom said as I slid into the booth next to him. Lorraine sat across from us twisting her hair around her finger and looking at the men in the room. I could see her giving eye contact to someone and I turned slightly to check it out. It was Mr. Demarie, the mailman. He was good looking but he was also almost old enough to be Lorraine's father.

"Watch it, Lorraine," I said, "Or they'll be vacuuming you off the backseat of some old Chevrolet."

"That's disgusting," Lorraine said and pushed her order of fried onion rings away. "I'm going to puke."

"God," Tom said. "That really was disgusting, Patsy!" His face was pale with shock. "You don't have to be so specific. Lorraine's not that kind of person."

"Right," I said. "Let's talk about how their radio was tuned to Randy's.'"

"I just thought it was interesting. That's the same station we listen to late at night."

"That's the station everyone listens to," Lorraine said.

"Thank you, Lorraine," I said, reaching out to pick up one of her onion rings. Just as I was about to take a bite, a small white-haired man came into the restaurant and paused in the doorway to stare down the row of booths.

"I know what you're all talking about!" he said loud enough for everybody to stop whatever they were doing and look at him. He, in turn, took the time to fix each person for an instant with his own look. He had a narrow face and huge white eyebrows like the wings of a moth over tiny, glaring black eyes.

"Oh my God," Lorraine said. "It's the minister from the church over in Bethel. He preached at our church once."

There was a sudden silence as the white-haired man raised his arms and said, "Remember Proverbs! 'Can a man take fire to his bosom, and his garments not be burned?'" Then he turned and walked out. A nervous laughter began and closed the gap he'd left.

I broke the crust of the onion ring with my teeth and let the flavor of the soft onion rest on my tongue. "I want to find the place where they parked."

"No you don't," Lorraine said. She gave Tom a pleading look, as if he might talk sense to me.

"It's miles away," Tom said. "Almost to the state line."

"You don't have to come," I said and stood up and dangled the keys to the ridiculous Studebaker in front of them.

She didn't. But Tom did. We took Little Savannah Road north for eleven miles and then turned east toward Mississippi and drove for another three or four miles on a narrow blacktop and then turned off on a gravel road through clay hills and pine woods. I had a map that the blue-haired waitress had drawn for me on a napkin.

We weren't the only ones on the trail. We followed a pickup through a cloud of red dust. The pickup turned off and wound along a logging road and then stopped in a clearing. There was another car already there, an old

Plymouth with a man and woman in the front seat. They started up the engine and drove away as soon as we pulled up. The two guys in the pickup stopped but kept the engine running and looked out of the window, the driver motioning and pointing. Then they drove off, too.

"It's just you and me," I said to Tom when the dust settled. I had turned off the engine. "And this is it."

"Yeah," he said softly and opened the door. He stepped out and looked around.

I got out my side. The sun had made the smell of pine strong like incense in the hot dry air. Cicada sounds grew and then died as we walked toward the edge of the clearing. Through the pines the leaves of a sweet gum tree flashed red as the sun angled down on it.

Tom sat on a log. I sat beside him.

"Why do you care about this so much?" he asked. It was a good question.

"I don't know. It just seems important."

"I don't understand. They were two people you didn't even know."

"It's real, Tom," I said, annoyed at this detachment. I almost wished Meat had let him look in the car. "What they did and what happened to them is real. It's the only thing in the whole world right now that seems real to me."

"What do you want from this?" he asked.

"To take fire to my bosom, Tom. Like the man said."

"You scare me," he said and got up and went back to the car. Neither of us spoke all of the way home.

"Tomorrow night," I said when I dropped him off.

That night I lay in my bed and listened through the walls for any sounds that might come from my parents' room. There never were any. Every night mother stayed up reading or sewing and my father went to bed early. At nine-thirty each night, my father went to the bathroom and brushed his teeth. Then he went to their room and put on his pajamas, read in bed for about ten minutes and then turned off the bed light. At ten-thirty or eleven, my mother turned off the lights in the living room and the kitchen and came upstairs to the bathroom, brushed her teeth, put Nivea cream on her face, and went into their bedroom. They never closed the door entirely, but left it open a crack so that if either my brother or I moaned in the night or tossed in our beds, we would instantly be heard and attended. The partially open door was to let us know that they lay in their bed on call. Whatever else they did in that bed they did in such cautious silence that I had grown to suspect that my brother and I were both adopted.

As I listened for my parents to make some sound, I thought about her, about the pink dress she left and the rabbit-fur jacket she wore. About eating cotton candy when she was stranded on the top of the Ferris wheel with a man whose wife and mother-in-law and children were all in church. Wondering why she was on the wheel at all, looking down at the light bulbs on the spokes, and the blurred faces of the crowd looking up, and wanting only to be with him in the dark and to touch him, wanting only to get back to earth and into the dark and touch him.

We were in Tom's mother's Buick on the backseat. It was Saturday night and we were parked in the clearing at the end of a logging road in the piney woods. We had turned the radio to "Randy's Record Shop," and it was playing rhythm and blues from some mountaintop in Tennessee. The heater was on but Tom had all four windows opened an inch. He would go along with me—but only so far.

We kissed. His arm was around me and I had my head up. I opened my mouth for his tongue. His free hand came up under my blouse and unhooked my brassiere. I unbuttoned his shirt and reached under his undershirt and felt skin. I slid my hands down and started on his belt buckle. He reached under my skirt and tugged on my panties. We got undressed quickly. I had the rubbers. I had taken them from my father's store. He kept them behind the counter so that people would have to ask for them.

In a minute Tom was sitting naked on top of me. Behind him two beams from the headlamps of an approaching car reached through the trees and found him. The beams struck his body and he became a silhouette with light flaring behind him like the pale flames from an eclipsed star. He shivered as if the flames were cold and I shivered too and then felt him inside of me. Then the lights went out and left us once more in the dark.

She was buried on Monday. I cut class and walked the six blocks from the school to the cemetery. I didn't want either Tom or Lorraine with me. There was only a handful of people at the graveside, but cars, driving extra slow, passed by almost constantly. It started to rain about halfway through the service, a cold sleety rain. I stood under a tree until the service was over and then I went home and went to bed.

He was buried the next day in a cemetery up at Bethel. I didn't go. There's only so much you can learn from things like this.

# The Realm of the Ordinary

WHEN I BROUGHT my aunt her groceries, she was on the phone to the cemetery—All Souls. It's an old one—though not the oldest—and the crypts of most of the families we know are there. This is New Orleans, you understand, and because the town is literally floating, we put our dead in tombs above the ground and wait for time, not worms, to do the job.

My aunt Liz is my mother's older sister, and, like my mother, she's small and feisty. "Well, how much does it cost to move bones from the upper level?" Liz said into the phone. It's an ancient wall phone and she had to stand on tiptoe to talk into it. For years she's had to stand on tiptoe to talk into the phone and that may account for the fact that she always sounds breathless and exasperated to whoever happens to be on the other end. I love Liz's voice. You could grate cheese with it.

I never appreciated the New Orleans accent, a combination of magnolia consonants and Brooklyn vowels, until now that I'm a thirty-six-year-old refugee from a dozen bland years in California. I'd gone west because I heard it never rained there and that mosquitoes and cockroaches were seen only in cameo appearances in horror movies. In California, I'd married, divorced, and held a series of jobs just good enough to delay what I'd always known would be my inevitable return to this soggy place.

"What do you mean, a coffin has to be biodegradable? That's soap, isn't it?" she said and motioned for me to sit down. "Listen, my niece Maggie is here. She does my shopping for me and I have to visit with her."

I began to unpack groceries, moving aside an almost empty bottle of Coca-Cola, an ashtray full of the twisted stumps of cigarettes, and a half-dozen glasses with various levels of the brown liquid in the bottoms. Liz hasn't had company. She just takes down a new glass whenever she has another drink of Coke. Toward the end of the day she washes up. She scowled as she listened. When she saw me looking at her she pointed to the phone and then twirled her index finger next to her temple. "You're an idiot," she said finally into the mouthpiece and slammed the earpiece into its stirrup.

"Who was that?" I asked.

"I'm moving Raymond's bones," she said. "Did you get Coke?"

I whipped out a big bottle and twisted off the cap. She reached into the freezer for a tray of ice and began to pop cubes into two fresh glasses.

"Raymond's bones?"

"I'm losing sleep over this." She sat and lit a Lucky with a kitchen match. "His sister Lucille is dying. She's got cancer and she's not going to make it. She's not going to want to be buried in Lake Charles. She's going to want to come back here and join the rest of the bunch."

"So?"

"So? So Raymond's on the top level now, but when Lucille dies, she'll get his place. That's the way it is. When someone dies, out goes the old coffin, in goes the new, and the latest bones get thrown in with the others down below. After that happens I'll never know which are his when I get our own crypt. You look at a pile of bones and how are you going to tell who's who?"

"I thought *you* were going to be buried in Raymond's family's crypt, too."

"I changed my mind."

I kept unpacking the bags and putting things away. Two packages of CDM coffee and chickory. Rice. Red beans. Ham hocks. Bologna. Pay Day candy bars. A carton of Luckies. Cinnamon rolls. Liz doesn't want to see anything green on her plate—not even parsley.

"I never liked his family and I'll be damned if I'm going to be buried in that crypt with them. They were nothing but snobs—all of them. His mother pretended she couldn't remember my name. She always called me Helene. That was a girlfriend of his from tenth grade. I didn't even like the way that family smelled." She tore open a bag of potato chips and began crunching them. She wasn't wearing her dentures and the ability to crunch without teeth seemed to calm her a bit.

This new preoccupation with death came as a surprise to me. Liz is the least sentimental human alive and, as far as I could remember, she had never even acknowledged mortality. After Raymond died, her primary mourning activity seemed to be reorganizing closet space.

"Do you have to do it right away?" I asked.

"After they shove Lucille in there, it's all over for Raymond." The fire on the end of the Lucky flared beneath her widened nostrils. "I'm moving his bones."

Raymond had been a short man, a dapper dresser in his day. Almost a dandy. He and Liz were quite a couple. There are pictures of them everywhere in the house. He in white linen. She a bride in a fancy wedding dress in spite of the Depression. It was a big wedding in Mater Dolorosa Church. His bones would be small bones, delicate. An anthropologist in the future would get the wrong idea of what we looked like if he had only Raymond's bones to go by.

"You're on Social Security," I said. "Do you have any idea how much a crypt costs?"

"We could buy one together," Liz answered, her bright-eyed slyness almost veiled by a puff of smoke.

"No," I said. "Car payments are bad enough. The present is all I can handle."

Liz slammed back her Coke the way someone would a shot of whiskey.

We weren't protected by a single cloud on the day Liz chose for our visit to the cemetery. The sun was fierce, and the city of the dead became a testing place for the living. Last night's rain turned to steam around our feet.

"It's awfully hot for May," I said. Liz gave me a look of scorn. Heat was part of the process of living in New Orleans, a component of *les bon temps*. Each time I complained about it to anyone in my family, that person looked at me with suspicion. Liz had an umbrella shading her. She'd offered me one when we left the house and I'd refused. I never felt right carrying an umbrella when it wasn't raining.

Liz had found the crypt—no mean feat considering the acres of unmarked trails between all those hundreds of buildings of white plastered brick. She stood mumbling the names inscribed on the rectangle of marble that sealed the entrance to the tomb. "Not one but Raymond worth a nickel," she said as I came closer. "I'm doing him a favor. Would you want to rise with that group? What do you think his mother's going to be wearing?"

It was a question I had never thought to contemplate—attire for the last really big party on earth.

"Not what she was buried in, I'll bet," Liz went on. "More like the dress she wore when she was queen of one of those balls—when they still had money." She rapped on the marble with her wedding ring. "Anybody home?" She grinned. She was wearing her dentures and they seemed too bright and new for her face. She rapped again and pretended to listen.

At the sound of this rapping a young man poked his head around from the shady side of the crypt and studied us. He had tight dark curls and skin the color of the Coca-Cola he held in one hand. In his other hand was half an oyster sandwich.

Liz looked up from her own pool of shade, startled, and then smiled with approval at the cola. "The real thing," she said.

He nodded, a solemn young man in a New Orleans Saints T-shirt and faded but recently pressed khaki slacks. His eyes were as pale as foam. "You ladies need something?" he asked, courteous, his voice ten degrees cooler than the day.

"Just money," Liz said.

"Ahhh, money," he said and took a bite of the sandwich. I watched his teeth close over the gold-crusted body of the oyster and watched him chew, a ruminant.

"We want to take out my uncle's bones and find another crypt for them—and for my aunt too—when she dies," I found myself saying. I'm not normally so forthcoming with strangers but his silence was like a vacuum cleaner sucking explanations.

Liz looked up at me over her shoulder, surprise lowering her jaw, revealing those glossy dentures. "That's about the size of it," she said. "The only thing standing in my way is money."

He swallowed and washed down the food with a large chug of cola. "I understand. I'm looking for work."

"Well, I'd like to help you, but I'd be hard pressed to get together ten cents for a shoe shine," she said.

He nodded, as though this were a perfectly reasonable position.

"Let's go," I said. Surrounded by the white walls of the crypts, I felt like something being cooked.

"Well, now you've seen it," Liz said to me and rapped once more on the marble. Then she looked up at the young man who was still standing there. "You did say you wanted work, didn't you?"

"I did," he said, as thoughtful as ever. "And I do."

"Give me something to write on, Maggie," she said. I found a scrap of paper, the back of a grocery receipt, and then a stub of pencil, and I watched her scribble away. "It's on the river side of the avenue."

He looked at the paper. "I'll find it," he said.

Back home, Liz propped the fan in front of an open window and put her feet on a chair. They were swollen like two small loaves of bread. Her face, without the dentures, had collapsed. She looked smaller than ever, and, for the first time I could remember, pitiful. "Tell me why I'm a foolish old woman," she said.

I poured Coke over ice and placed the glass in her hand. "You're a foolish old woman because whatever happens after your death—or Raymond's death—isn't important."

"Why don't I believe that?" she asked.

"I've done this before," he said. I held the beam of light on a huge screwdriver that seemed like an extension of his right forefinger, a wand. Barely an hour earlier, Liz had wakened me with a summons to her house because Jean Felice—that was his name—said he needed someone to drive him. He and I now stood in front of Raymond's family crypt. I half expected clouds to roll over and lightning to streak.

"What do you mean?" I asked. I wasn't sure that I liked any of this, and I wasn't made more comfortable by the knowledge that I was with a pro.

"So many ladies get lonely for their men—for their dear departed. They want them back in their lives. I help the poor widows. You wouldn't believe how many lonely widows there are."

The night was damp—and cool—but not cold enough for the chill that crept up my back. This was more than an eccentric errand for a distressed relative. I was robbing a grave. And all because when I'd walked into Liz's house just moments ago, I'd been unable to resist the sight of her—elated, her hair red once more and crackling with sparks—dancing around the kitchen with Jean Felice.

From beyond the cemetery walls came the rattle of streetcar wheels on track. I had no idea they ran so late—or so early. "What do you mean, you do this a lot?"

"Oh, not a lot," he said, his voice low and as reassuring as I wanted it to be. "Just enough."

As he began to remove the top-right screw, the beam of light began to jump like the bouncing ball in an old movie sing-along.

"Have you given a thought to the final place for you and yours?" he asked in a steadying tone.

"I'm divorced. I probably won't even know where his bones are buried. Or his ashes strewn. Or whatever."

"Oh," Jean Felice said, and I couldn't miss the disappointment in his voice. Losing track of a loved one, or even a once-loved one, I realized, must have seemed to him like a betrayal, or, at least, a failure. I stifled the desire to apologize as he placed a screw in his shirt pocket.

"Hold the light here," he said and pointed to the last screw, in the top-left corner. I watched him take it out, then lower his large frame into a squat, the kind that people who know how to work get into when there's something heavy to be lifted. He placed one hand on each side of the slab of marble. "I can do this by myself," he said. "Just open the suitcase."

The suitcase was the largest member of a set of three hard-sided Samsonite pieces that Liz had won in a raffle at Mater Dolorosa. Raymond was dead when she won it. It had never been used before. I opened the satiny lining to the night sky.

"Perhaps you'd better look away," he said. "Put the flashlight down by the suitcase."

I didn't protest. I not only looked away but took several steps in a direction that led me away. From that position I heard scraping, banging, sliding, and finally a clattering, which was a dry sound like a whisper. "Nice bones," Jean Felice said. "Tidy bones."

Liz had fresh coffee and stale doughnuts waiting for us. It was clear to me as soon as I saw her face, its mixture of apprehension and expectation, that she'd had no idea what to hope for, that she'd been driven by a fear that as soon as Lucille died, Raymond, in some way only she could understand, would be lost to her. "Oh, sweet

Jesus," she said when she saw the suitcase. "Is he...?" She took a step forward and then stopped.

"He's resting inside," Jean Felice said and put the suitcase at her feet just as a porter at the depot would have.

She made no move to pick it up.

"Would you like me to shake it?" he asked.

"Oh no," she said, backing away, her hand on her heart.

"Just where do you want it, Liz?" I asked. I wasn't finding this much easier than she was, but Liz's domain was, after all, the realm of the ordinary, and I wanted to call her back to it. She turned toward me, flustered but relieved.

"There's space in my bedroom closet," she said. Jean Felice picked up the suitcase and together we followed her into the cluttered room. She opened the door to the closet and took out a pile of blankets wrapped in a clear plastic bag. "Right there," she said. Jean Felice slid the suitcase into the space and closed the door.

"I can't thank you enough," Liz said when he stood facing her, dusting his hands. "I'm afraid I was about to go crazy."

"Not at all," he said and bowed his head.

"What can I give you for your troubles?" she asked.

This question astonished me. I couldn't believe she hadn't talked about this before, but then I realized that she'd been in such a state of frantic anticipation that thoughts of money had just slipped away. I had a brief vision of Jean Felice retrieving the suitcase from the closet and holding it hostage to some extravagant demand.

"Whatever you'd like," he said, eyes down.

Liz grabbed me by the arm and pulled me to the side of

the room, pressing me against an armoire. "What do you have?" she said, and then followed me to the kitchen where I'd left my handbag. I had a ten, a five, and four ones.

"I have nineteen dollars."

"That'll be fine," he said. "I'll take fifteen and leave you with the ones, and tell your aunt I'll be looking for a suitable crypt for her." He put the money away, then reached over and took my hand, examined it, then squeezed it. "You're a good person. You're going to make nice bones too someday."

"Thank you," I said.

Liz and I watched him walk down the porch stairs. The rising sun cast long shadows and Jean Felice's slid along the ground after him. As soon as he turned the corner, Liz went back in and opened the refrigerator. "It's too hot for coffee," she said, dropping ice into two glasses, the smile on her face positively goofy with joy.

"It is." I was tired suddenly, my eyes heavy.

"Could you stop at the grocery after work?" she asked, pouring in the Coke. "I'm all out of a few things."

"Of course, " I said, watching her set the full glass on the table. She had begun to hum, something off-key and wheezy. As I reached for the glass, I took a look at my hand—at the scar on my middle finger from a cut when I was ten, at the pattern of freckles on the back, at the alphabet of tiny lines creasing my palm—at the clever skin. "Whatever you need."

# Three Rivers

THE MAN SIMONE D'QUESNAY had been engaged to marry was shot and killed on a Normandy beach. One year later, despite her grief—or because of it—she married Alex Oliver, a distant cousin from north Louisiana. For a while she seemed happy, but then she began to do things that were hard to understand.

People in town excused her at first. They said that she had tragedy on her side, that she wasn't able to get over Jackie Hebert's death, and they were inclined to feel sorry for her. But their pity started to wear thin. The sky blue Packard convertible that Jackie had given Simone as an engagement present was turning up in odd places, and Simone, as she drove daily, methodically, over the back roads of St. Athanatius Parish, grew more and more careless about whom she was seen with.

At first it had been Alex's Aunt TaTa. Well, if a young and beautiful woman like Simone wanted to drive around with an old crone, who could find fault with that? TaTa obviously loved riding. She held her little black straw hat on with one white-gloved hand and used the other hand to point to things they passed as she named them. "Pussy cat. Post office. Little pissant." Taking particular delight in each pop of a *p* and hiss of an *s*.

Sometimes, the cook's half-wit daughter Ophelia occupied the front seat beside Simone. Ophelia rode with her head back and her mouth open, her upturned eyes like dark marbles in a bowl.

Later, the long-boned, gap-toothed adolescent Felton Mackay rode alongside Simone. Felton, who worked at the gas station, was known to be part of a inbred clan from up by the state line, a group rumored to make a living by supplying two-headed calves and hump-backed mules for traveling sideshows.

"She talks a streak," Felton said to his boss after one ride. "She took me to some little church in Savannah Branch and made me sit there while she prayed—on her knees! I didn't have no notion of what she was saying on the way out—or the way back."

"Are you going to put gas in her car or am I?" asked Mole, the owner of the station. Simone was pacing in the shade of the awning. Her peach-colored linen dress, damp with sweat from sitting on the leather upholstery, clung to her legs as she followed a line between two slabs of concrete, placing one high-heeled shoe in front of the other like a tightrope walker.

"I'm only all right when I'm driving," Simone said.

"Uhhuun," Ophelia moaned.

"As soon as I leave a place there's this sense of relief. And then, of course, there's anticipation about what I'll find at the next place. Then when I get there I can't wait to get away and go somewhere else."

Ophelia moaned again, bringing up two fingers to her lips. Simone reached into her bag and took out a pack of Herbert Taryinton's, lit two cork-tipped cigarettes, and handed one to Ophelia. The Packard bounced over a wooden bridge and Ophelia giggled. "Your mother doesn't like my giving you cigarettes," Simone said and smiled when Ophelia grinned, the plume of smoke leaving the girl's lips like a feathery substitute for a word.

Then someone new appeared on the seat of the Packard beside Simone. To her credit, Simone at first seemed to be trying to act with discretion, but Marigny was a small town and, at best, discretion could be only a holding action.

He fixed cars. There had been something wrong with the Packard and he was recommended to Simone. He raised the hood and bent over the world of metal and spark that the hood protected her from knowing. She watched as his grease-stained arms, ropy muscled and quick, moved in and out. A wrench here. Turning something there. His fingers prodded and probed. He sat on the creamy leather and touched the wheel that only she touched. He turned the key and listened.

"It was your carburator," he said. "I think I've fixed it. You shouldn't have any more trouble."

"No," she said.

His name was Ruben Fouchet and his auto shop was under a raised house that sat among others like it—shabby buildings all—on a spit of dredged-up mud and shell on the other side of the bayou. In the rooms above, his wife had a business. The painted wooden sign at the end of the driveway read FRANCINE'S BEAUTY SHOPPE. A sign in the top half of the window advertised permanent waves. Pink cafe curtains hung over the bottom half.

Simone wrote him a check. He folded it without even glancing at it and then he placed his hand on her waist and looked at her.

"I'll be out at Three Rivers on Friday night," he said.

When Simone got home, she took off the lilac linen dress and saw that his fingers had made a black print at the waist. She folded the dress and placed it in a box with tissue paper and put it on a shelf.

Three Rivers Pavilion was a long, screened dance hall at the end of a road reached by crossing an arching white-timbered bridge. The pavilion overlooked a wide expanse of water, almost a small lake, created by the convergence of three slow-moving rivers. On one end were tables where people sat and drank and ate boiled shrimp and crab. At the other end was a dance floor and a band.

She and Ruben were like one body as they whirled around the floor. They were both tall and slender with dark hair and pale eyes—his blue, hers green. Simone wore a yellow dress and he a blue shirt and black slacks. Anyone watching—and there were many—could see how much Simone loved being held by him.

How soon Alex heard about this affair was open to question. Alex was aloof, something of a recluse—a snob, perhaps. He wasn't the sort of person just anyone could go up to and say, "I saw your wife with a Cajun grease monkey at a dance hall the other night. She looked damp enough to pour in a glass and drink down straight."

She had her life, and Alex had his studies. He read history, especially the history of battles. That summer he was reading about the Punic Wars. Simone was happy to point out to him, whenever the subject came up, that his interest in things seemed to be inversely proportional to their distance from him in time or space. As they receded from him, he became fascinated.

They ate lunch together most days at a round wicker

table on the big front porch with a view through the trees of the lake. Sometimes Alex would bring a book to the table and sometimes he would also bring in a yellow legal pad on which he'd make sketches of some action or another. He'd eat a bit, take a sip of his iced tea, read, and then jot down some position. After each notation he'd raise his head and lift his farsighted eyes to Simone to let her know that conversation could take place.

"We could drive up to Vicksburg and visit a real battleground," she'd say. "I realize it's not Carthage or Rome, but we could sit on real ground that has almost recently been stained by real blood. It's just a hop, skip, and a jump away. We could go to Chalmette—that's almost next door—and look for cannonballs in the bushes."

"You drive anywhere you want," he'd say. "Leave me out of it."

"We took this very drive the day before Jackie left for Europe," Simone said to Ophelia. "We didn't understand the smallest thing then." They were driving over a white shell road through miles of shoulder-high marsh grass. "Of course, I'd be married to him, but would that make any real difference? Would I be doing what I'm doing if Jackie hadn't been killed? Would I be restless like this?"

Ophelia took her chewing gum out of her mouth and examined it.

"Just remember not to stare at the sun," Simone said. "You could go blind. That would just about do it for you." She took a sip of Coke and passed the bottle to the girl. "I'm thinking strange thoughts, Ophelia. A friend of mine's father jumped off the Huey P. Long Bridge and was swept down the river for miles before they dragged him out. He drowned, of course, and it has never ceased to distress his family. Hunting accidents are often suicide—when they aren't murder. I can't imagine a bullet piercing my skull, though, can you? I try to imagine it—the moment of impact. So sudden. Then what? A great big hole full of light?"

Ophelia passed her back the bottle and Simone took a swallow. "It's just morbid, I know."

Her visits to churches around the countryside continued. There probably wasn't a single church, of any denomination, that Simone hadn't prayed in. "If you go to Mass on the first Friday of each month for seven months, God has promised that he won't let you die without a chance to confess," Simone told Felton Mackay.

"We don't hold with confession in my church."

"Well, if you plan on sinning, it's a good idea to have confession."

"I have to get back to work now," he said. "Besides, I don't plan on sinning."

"Good for you," she said. "Maybe you should pray for me then."

"Yes, Ma'am," he said and looked out his side of the car. Later Felton told Mole that he didn't think he'd ride with her anymore, even though she'd never been anything but nice and he did admire the car.

"You know, I don't remember much about him. Mostly I remember the way he smelled. He smelled like expectation. He was killed in the war," Simone said. She was standing by a window of a cabin that Ruben had brought her to. The river outside was pale in the moonlight. Ruben sat on a cot behind her smoking.

"So he's dead and you aren't?" he said.

"Maybe that's all there is to it. Maybe I feel I should be dead, too."

"Maybe? What else could there be?

"I can't believe it's only that. When I was little I used to pray that I'd become a saint. Only I didn't want to be a saint to be good. I wanted to be a saint to be lifted up off the earth when I prayed. I remember praying in chapel and expecting at any moment for at least an inch of airspace to appear between my knees and the wood." She turned around to see if he was listening. The only light in the room besides the red stump of his cigarette came from a kerosene lamp on a chest of drawers. His eyes never left her. "There are words that make me crazy when I hear them," she said. "There are words I almost can't bear to hear—words like *rapture,* and *frenzy,* and *transport.*"

"What will you settle for?" he asked.

She poured some bourbon into a glass and took a sip. "That's really it, isn't it?"

"We don't get many choices, *cher.*"

"We could be dead."

"My father drowned," he said. "Can you imagine that, a man from the bayou drowning? I mean, my people don't drown. God gave us webbed feet like ducks, you know."

"So what happened?"

"I guess he forgot how to swim."

"What do you think of this place?" she asked. She had invited Ruben to come driving with her the next day. It was a day so hot that as soon as they turned off the highway and stopped, they were covered with a film of moisture. She had pulled onto a dirt road to park under an oak tree near a tiny house that had been turned into a church. Someone had crawled onto the roof and fashioned a steeple on the peak out of pieces of an old crate. The panes of the windows were painted in checkered patterns of purple and gold.

Simone pushed open the door and led the way. It was cool inside. There was a kitchen table covered with flowered oilcloth for the altar and seven pews. The light through the windows made the room look like a neon-lit aquarium.

"I think this is a crazy place," he said, "but I like it."

"Me too," she said. She sat in a pew and bowed her head for a moment. "The minister here is just the holiest man—all gnarled and bent over," she whispered after a bit. "I think he was born in slavery. He's so old and his voice is just always about to break but I came one Sunday for the services and, let me tell you, when that wheezy organ in the corner there started, that little old man sang like he was expecting to be heard directly in heaven."

"Did you sing too?" he asked.

"Oh no," she said and crossed her legs and straightened her skirt. "I was just a guest in a sacred place."

Back outside, the day was even hotter than before. The sun boring through the branches of the oaks seared white smoky patches on the grass.

"I'd like to leave a little offering," Simone said, opening her handbag and taking out her gold compact. She walked over to one of the brick foundation piers, picked up a twig, knelt, dug a hole next to the pier, and buried the compact. Ruben stood back and watched her. "There," she said and dusted off her hands.

"Is that it?" he asked.

"For now," she said.

"I'm tolerant, Simone, but I'm no fool," Alex said the next day at lunch. He put aside his yellow pad and looked in her direction. She had been going through the personal section of the *Times-Picayune* circling ads that thanked St. Jude for favors received.

"St. Jude is the two-to-one favorite over all," she said. "He even beats out the Blessed Mother. Hopeless cases, you understand. The city must be full of them."

"I have heard talk from such disparate sources as Billy Friedrichs, my lawyer, and Mole Guidry, who services my car."

"I'm trying to understand things, Alex."

"I'm not thrilled about being on the apex of a triangle."

"I'm truly sorry, Alex, to hurt you." She pulled a shrimp from the crown of tomato on her plate and then put it back. "I know this isn't what you need to hear, but, really, this doesn't have anything to do with you."

"I'm going to try to be patient, Simone. I care for you. I worry."

"I am praying, you know, Alex. I'm not happy either."

The kerosene lamp on the end of the pier cast a flickering light on the water and they swam to it. Ruben crawled out first and squatted on the wood and pulled her up so they could lie like two silvery fish on the weathered boards.

"I don't understand how a person could forget how to swim," she said.

"No, me neither. When my mama heard about my

daddy, she ran off the pier in front of the house and jumped in the water, but she bobbed to the top like a cork. Maybe she wanted to forget, but she couldn't."

Simone sighed and rolled over. He reached to touch her, but she pulled away. "I want to go back and dance," she said. "Let's go back to the pavilion."

"This all . . . what we're doing, can't go on much longer, Simone."

"I know." She stood and walked to the cabin.

He held her that night when they danced as if he expected not to hold her again. She kept her arms around him, her body against his. When the music stopped, they stood side by side under the colored lanterns and looked over the place where the rivers came together. When the music started, they danced again, legs and arms like limbs reflected in a mirror.

Later that night, rather than drive directly to Marigny from Three Rivers, they chose to detour on a lonely road that led through stretches of logged-over land. Ruben leaned back, his eyes closed. When she swerved and he felt the gravel under the tires, his whole body jerked up.

"What was that?" she asked him after straightening the car. "Did you see it? There was something in the road, something big and dark. It was waiting for me." Her voice shook.

"I didn't see anything," he said. "It was probably a deer. The headlights get them sometimes and they can't move."

"It was something big," she said and then she let out her breath—as if she'd been holding it for a long time. "I just don't want to kill anything."

"Well, whatever it was, you didn't hit it."

"Oh," she said. "Don't let me kill anything."

"Let me drive, *cher.*" He reached for the wheel, but she pushed his hand away.

"No, I can't let you. This is what I do."

She started laughing, then singing, then shouting, "We're gonna fly, Ruben, honey! They can't keep us here! We're going to lift off the ground." She pressed the gas and they sped forward, the only car on the road with nothing but the dark stunted forest stretching away on either side. There was a sudden crack in the sky in front of them and a wide jagged door of light opened. "There it is," she cried. "There it is!" Then the thunder broke and the rain, a seamless sheet of water, covered the open car.

Almost every light in the house was burning when Simone got back. Usually after dinner Alex went to his study to read and left on only the front-porch light for her. That night he came out onto the porch and stood blocking the door. He wore a silk robe over his pajamas. His eyes had rings under them and there were new hollows in his cheeks.

"Alex!" Simone said. She pushed back her soaking wet hair, lifted her chin, and met his eyes, "How nice of you to come out to greet me!"

"There is no pleasure involved," he said. "Someone has come to see me, someone you should take into consideration." He stepped aside and let her pass him and walk into the hall.

In the living room, on the edge of the Aubusson rug, stood a small birdlike woman in a much-washed flowered dress. She stood beside one of the long windows facing the lake, a hand placed lightly against the glass.

"Oh, dear God . . ." Simone said.

"You do know who I am, don't you?" the woman said. Her voice was low, and she spoke slowly, as if control were important and a great deal at stake.

Simone nodded. "Yes, I know." She raised her hands as if there were something in them that she could offer and then let them drop to her sides. "I'm just sorry." She brushed past Alex, and walked back the way she'd come. A moment later the engine of the Packard started and Simone pulled away from the house. She still hadn't put up the top.

She didn't return until the next afternoon. She'd had her hair done and she was wearing a new dress. She wore new sunglasses too, which she didn't remove. Alex was waiting for her at the top of the steps.

"I'm relieved to see you, Simone."

"I don't seem to be able to do anything but apologize these days, Alex. I'm sorry," she said and gave him her hand, which he took and held as if it were the only part of her he could hold on to.

"I'm sorry too, Simone. I called everywhere. Where were you?"

"I drove to Mississippi." She sighed, a long exhausted sigh. "And to be perfectly honest, Alex, I have no idea why. I didn't pass a damn thing on the road but snake farms, Holy Roller tabernacles, and gas stations with albino sharecroppers selling white lightning out of the trunks of cars."

"What are you going to do?"

"I don't know. I really don't." She took her hand from his and went into the kitchen, where Ophelia was slowly breaking the ends from green beans.

"Let's take a ride, Ophelia. I want company. Let's take us a little ride."

They drove along the lake where clouds were building again in the south, gray clouds that pressed down. There was no breeze. They drove to the dredged-out bayou and up to the house on pilings. Any cars that had been there before were gone. The sign that said FRANCINE'S BEAUTY SHOPPE was gone.

Ophelia stumbled up the steps after Simone, who pushed open the door. In the front room was a hair dryer, a mirror, a basin, and a beauty-parlor chair. The floor was linoleum and scarred. Pink paper decorated with poodles, balloons, and scenes of Paris covered the walls. The paper looked newer than anything else in the room, as if once, fairly recently, someone had tried for a fresh start. Bottles and magazines and combs and curlers and clothing were scattered everywhere. A wind might have been blowing through that room for days. Behind was a kitchen with dishes in the sink and food on plates and a bag of rotting garbage by the rear door. In the bedroom the double bed was stripped and empty hangers dangled in the closet.

"I never wanted things to turn out like this," Simone said. She took Ophelia's hand to prevent her from touching anything as they walked through the rooms, almost as if Simone expected some future inventory in which the whole scene would need to be exhibited unviolated. "You have to believe that."

A few minutes later Simone pulled the Packard into the driveway of her own house. "Go on back in," she said. "Your mother will be expecting you." She waited while Ophelia got out and trotted up to the house. As soon as she could see the girl on the porch, Simone drove away.

A fine rain began to fall as she rounded the bend that marked the final mile. Ahead, the arching bridge rose, its crisscrossed wooden timbers white against the green trees beyond.

She was gathering speed so that when she hit the railings, the car broke through as if on course, as if the railings were part of the way it had to travel. The Packard left the bridge and found nothing but air beneath its tires. As the car waited in space, Simone, still at the wheel, hovered with it, suspended for an instant. Then car and driver plunged into the water.

Instead of sinking immediately, the Packard floated downstream like a gay blue boat until it filled and disappeared. A man in a skiff pulled Simone from the river.

"What were you trying to do?" he asked.

"I just wanted to hang there," she said. "I never wanted to drown."

# Life Signs

LINDA MARTIN SIPS her second beer of the afternoon and watches the brown pelicans fly in a staccato line across the eastern horizon. Right before they get to a large rock that juts out into the water, they break file and dive, bringing in their wide wings and dropping like stones.

"Are you sure you're all right—comfortable?" her husband Bob asks. He has finished leveling their travel trailer on the spot she has chosen on this Mexican beach.

"I'm an indolent, not an invalid," she says from her folding lounge chair and lifts her Dos Equis in a toast to him.

"Don't you want a pillow or your bird book or your binoculars?" he asks.

"No, thank you. They're pelicans—brown ones. I can see that from here."

"Are you sure that everything is fine?"

"Yes," she answers, smiling. "I'm really fine."

He shrugs and smiles back, as if he's not completely convinced, and then begins to do what he always does when they arrive at a new beach in Mexico—clean up. Out of the corner of her eye, Linda sees him, shirtless and tan, and only slightly paunchy in his old cutoffs, bending over and over again, picking up litter and placing it in one of his large green plastic bags.

Past Bob, beyond a spill of rocks, toward the curving arm of the little bay, a figure walks with a dog along the water's edge. Because of the distance and the failing light, Linda can't be sure if the two are coming or going. She turns her attention back to the pelicans. She remembers reading that only a few years ago they were threatened with extinction. The *E* word. Now they are back in numbers. It is something to be happy about, this return from the brink. She toasts them! Lucky survivors.

As the sun slides down behind her, lighting only the tips of the dusty palm trees, she faces the Sea of Cortez and tries to imagine that she is Eve, landed in some pristine Eden. She makes an effort to believe that the litter and the mangy, possibly rabid dogs that lurk just beyond the pale of beer cans, plastic bottles, used batteries, and disposable diapers do not exist.

She is not as good as pretending as she once was, a discovery she has recently made about herself—one of many recent discoveries. Ever since that doctor in an office as glossy and impersonal as an airline terminal told her that she had not passed the clean-bill-of-health test, Linda has felt that she's on a runaway train, plowing through all the little fictions she'd erected and assumed would endure. The first to collapse was the notion that she was in control of her own body.

"We can offer you several alternatives, several options," the doctor had said. "We will not remove so much chest muscle...take fewer lymph nodes...less discomfort...reduce the possibility of swelling in your arm...radiation...chemotherapy."

The words were a litany she knew he had chanted many times. His voice rose and fell implausibly and his eyes never met hers. Then the nurse came in and he went out.

"I'm only forty-five," she said to the nurse. "Does this happen often?"

"It happens," the nurse answered.

That night she slowly took off her clothes in front of the hospital-room mirror, touching her body cautiously, as she would touch the body of a stranger she'd been asked to undress. The next morning she went into surgery.

Bob returns dragging a full green sack. He ties it up and then opens the storage compartment of the trailer, where he keeps the inflatable craft.

"Will you be needing help with the boat?" she asks.

"No," he replies. "I got this model so I could do it alone." As soon as he says this, he looks stricken, realizing it's too late to call back the words. "You know what I mean," he says lamely.

She waves her hand as if waving away a fly. "Not to worry. I never did like boats anyway."

The boat is new. Bob had wanted one like it for years, but only last month, after they had spent two awful weeks camping in the parking lot of a clinic in Tijuana, could she finally persuade him to buy it. "Listen," she said, "I don't believe in this damn laetrile business, and I know I don't want to spend my last days sitting around with a lot of other dying people. Let's do what we always said we'd like to do," she begged. "Let's explore Baja, camp on the beach—fish! For God's sake!"

So here they are.

"What are you using for bait?" she asks. Even though she honestly doesn't like boats, or throwing out fishing lines, or fooling with hooks, the little subtleties of fishing intrigue her. She has enjoyed catching insects on the banks of rivers, seeing what their hatch is and trying to imitate it with various bits of colored fluff.

"If you promise not to tell those purists back home," he says.

She crosses her heart and holds up her Girl Scout fingers.

"Live bait!" he grins. "I'm into serious meat hunting tonight."

He drags the boat to the water's edge, pumps air into it, and mounts the motor. A stray pelican lands a few feet away and waddles tentatively to the bait bucket. Bob reaches into the bucket and throws a fish to the pelican, who catches it. Linda claps and Bob bows as if he's part of a clever act. Then he pulls the boat through the small surf and heads in a southerly direction. The motor makes an optimistic noise. The orange boat looks jaunty and indomitable.

The figures down the beach grow larger. A woman with short, curly blonde hair comes toward her. A large German shepherd is at her heels. The woman waves like someone flagging a car and Linda reluctantly waves back. She has been almost happy watching the little orange blob bounce across the water and she doesn't want to encourage company. But her answering wave is enough. The woman approaches.

"Hi there, neighbor!" the woman says boisterously, walking right up to Linda. The dog, an old one with milky eyes and a failing hip, settles down at the woman's feet. "Mind if I sit?"

Linda shrugs. She saw it coming. It's too late now to object. "Sure, have a seat."

The woman sinks onto the other lounge chair. "I saw you guys heading in. I was watching you get your trailer down that rocky little road. I'll bet you didn't see our RV over there in that palm grove until you got all the way down."

In fact, they hadn't. Linda and Bob thought they would have the beach to themselves.

"We've been here for a week and we're ready for company," the woman says. She kicks off her red plastic sandals and puts up her feet. "My companion gets bored so easily. He's a Libra, you understand. I think they're sort of shallow. I'm a double Scorpio myself, and you know what that means."

"Well, really, I don't. I'm a little vague about astrology," Linda says. She badly wants another beer, but to get up and get one without offering the woman something would be rude.

"I never get bored," the blonde woman continues. "I have my psychic studies." She moves her lips in a way that might be a smile. She has large teeth that overlap in a tiny mouth. Her features are small and seem to float on a round, almost-pretty, face. Linda decides that the woman is about her own age—but looks younger. She smiles back and lets her eyes fall to the woman's breasts, which are tan and firm and full above the low neckline of a pale blue tank top. As soon as she realizes she's staring, Linda forces her eyes back up to the woman's face.

"I'm just fascinated by psychic phenomena," the woman is saying. Her eyes are bright, like miniature Christmas tree lights.

"I've never given it much thought," Linda says, and stands. Her thirst has gotten the better of her. "I have some beer in the fridge. Would you like one?"

"Sure, honey, whatever you're having. I'm a tequila girl myself. Te-qui-la!"

"Right!" Linda calls from the doorway. What the hell! Have a beer. The country from whose borne no traveler returns. Or something like that. What had the doctor said? He'd been vague. A year... more or less... who knows. And when had he said it? Thanksgiving. She cooked a turkey with all the trimmings and the children had dutifully come home from school, but neither she nor Bob could really talk to them. She just stuffed them with food and cried after they left. Now it is March. She flips off the bottle caps. Foam pours out of the narrow brown necks and over her fingers. "Tequila!"

Linda holds a cold beer in each hand and does a little dance step on the sandy linoleum, then goes out.

"Sorry, no tequila," she says, handing the woman the beer. "Tomorrow in Loreto we'll pick up some tequila."

"And limes," the woman says.

"And limes." Linda wants music. She goes back into the trailer and slips a cassette into the stereo and comes back out. It is Neil Young singing about how rock and roll will never die.

"Shit! I love that song," the woman says. "I grew up in Anaheim. Rock and roll was religion. That was before Disneyland."

"Right, Anaheim. We drove through Anaheim," Linda says, and sits. "So tell me about this psychic business. What have I been missing?"

"I used to be a handmaiden in the Court of King Arthur. I wore these big gold bracelets. I saw it all in a hypnotic trance years ago." The woman stretches out her arms, turning them in and out as if looking for the missing bracelets.

"That's pretty amazing," Linda says. She can still see a small orange speck out on the water. Bright orioles catch the light as they fly to the palm trees behind the trailer.

"It was a very wealthy court. I was on speaking terms with Merlin."

"Really? Merlin?"

"I've named my dog after him. Merlin." The dog, hearing its name repeated, looks up expecting something.

"Loyal," Linda says. The east is almost dark now; the rock with the pelicans is a black spot against the sky.

"And then I was Charlotte Corday," the woman says, putting down an empty bottle.

"You always seemed to run with a fast crowd."

"Yeah, that's me. Maybe we have some tequila at our place. No. No, we drank it up last night. It goes down too easy. Margaritas, you know. I make a mean margarita."

"Well, tell me more about that stuff," Linda says. Her own beer tastes better than ever. She doesn't even want tequila. "I wonder why I've never been interested in all of that. I never even read Jeane Dixon."

"I find that hard to believe. I can't believe anybody's not interested!"

"Well," Linda says, "maybe I should be. Who knows?" She drinks more beer and looks out at the water. She now has a slight buzz. Mexican beer is stronger. Who ever knows?

"I've always been fascinated. Past lives are only one interest of mine." The woman settles back. Her voice has an agreeable harshness. "Great blondes in history. That's another interest I have. The night Marilyn died I had this terrible sense that something was wrong. I felt very connected to her."

"But do you really believe it? I mean, what makes you so sure that some part of you isn't just inventing it to please some other part?" Her beer is no longer sitting well. She feels an itching annoyance now.

"Honey, I have read hundreds of books, but mostly it's gut feeling." The woman says this and pounds her stomach with a fist. "Gut feeling!"

"Oh," Linda says. "Well, I just don't feel it—anywhere."

"If you want to be that way, go on and be that way," the woman says.

"It's not how I want to be," Linda says. "I'm not how I want to be. Wanting has nothing to do with anything." She pulls up her loose blouse and exposes her specially made brassiere. "Look!"

The woman looks with a puzzled, fuzzy expression.

"No, that isn't it," Linda says, and pulls up the brassiere. Beneath it lies a too-pink scar—as if nobody has even tried to be neat. "They didn't get it. That's what the doctor said. Like getting a joke or something."

"Wow," says the woman slowly. "I've never seen a scar like that before. It's not pretty."

"That's just the surface. The really ugly stuff is going on inside of me."

"Well, they have all kinds of places here in Mexico—like the place where Steve McQueen . . ."

"Died," Linda interrupts, lowering her blouse. In the silence she can hear the orioles rattling around in the palms. She must have forgotten to rewind the tape.

"Don't take it so hard," the woman says. "Look at it this way. You're going to come back."

"As a famous blonde, perhaps?"

"That, I don't know."

"Well, neither do I," Linda says, and sighs. "I think I need to be alone."

"I hear you, honey. Sure, take it easy. It's time for me

and Merlin here to toddle on home anyway. My companion will be looking inside the refrigerator trying to figure out how to turn stuff in plastic packages into food. Cheers!"

"Cheers!"

When the woman is gone, Linda goes into the trailer for another beer. She feels foolish, mean spirited, downright rude. The woman was only trying to be friendly. She shouldn't let things get to her so. Past lives, coming back over and over again—somehow it seems to miss the point.

On the counter is her tattered *Field Guide to Western Birds*. She leafs through it, looking at all her neat notes in the margins, all the small black check marks on the Life List pages. It is becoming quite a good list. Just yesterday she had walked up a dry riverbed, stepping carefully over the rounded stones, and came upon a wild confusion of hummingbirds sipping at the white trumpet-flowered bushes. She saw black-fronted hummers for the first time, and the familiar rufous ones she fed in her garden at home. Then last night Bob suggested that they take the ferry across to Puerto Vallarta so that she could look for parrots in the jungle there.

She closes the book and takes out a beer, then rips open a bag of corn chips. She used to love corn chips. Now they make her queasy. She crunches one between her teeth anyway. Pretty soon she'll probably have to give up beer. She decides against music and goes outside to sit.

The orioles in the palms gradually quiet down. The only sound comes from the road up behind the beach, where an occasional truck shifts gears for the next upgrade. A flattened circle of moon appears. The pelicans on the rock are still—turned to stone for all she can tell.

In a while she hears the sound of the engine. Then it

quits and she sees the dark shape that is Bob wading through the surf, dragging the boat onto the sand. There is such a happy energy in his movements. He is so alive. She finds herself angry with him. For the bounce in his step. For his enthusiasm for fishing. For his relentless cheerfulness. When he has the boat beached, he comes trotting up to the circle of light outside the trailer door. He is holding a large fish on a gaff in front of him.

"Get the charcoal ready!" he says. He grins and waves the fish in front of her, then kneels beside her and grabs her around the waist with his free arm.

"Get that thing out of my face!" she says, but he continues to dangle it there. He leans to her and nibbles her neck and kisses her right below her ear, and then on her shoulder. She finally laughs because she knows how much he wants her to. He tightens his grip on her and brings the fish even closer. It shines silver, with the iridescent blue and brilliant flecks of gold. It is so bright and his breath on her neck is so warm. She can't tell him how hard he is making it for her.

# UFO

THE MAN BEN and I had come to meet was busy swimming laps through the fluorescent green water of the motel pool. Above that glowing rectangle, the night sky glowed too, neon orange fading to neon pink. Barstow, Hub-of-the-Mojave.

After ten minutes or so, Chuck pulled himself out of the pool and made his way toward us, which was a relief since Ben had almost shattered the glass top of our table, knocking one of its legs with his impatient, jerking knee. Each time the table wobbled I glared at Ben, and each time he looked back, surprised and apologetic, and began polishing his head with his stubby fingers. At sixty, Ben was as chubby, pink, and hairless as a baby—and as trusting.

"You'll tell your great-grandchildren about this night," Chuck said before either of us had a chance to say anything. As he spoke he rubbed his chest with a towel as if trying to massage the huge bald eagle tattooed there, a wing spread over each of his hairy pectorals. His words, aimed at Ben, dropped as neatly as a caddis fly on a stream and Ben rose like a trout.

"Yes, Ben," Chuck intoned, "I'm glad you made it. I'm not sure if you realize it, but only a few minutes from the very place where we now sit Dwight David Eisenhower met with the leader of an alien force from outer space. The leader assumed a human form for the occasion, of course. It was historic but, you understand, Ben, that Ike couldn't tell anyone, or mass hysteria would result. Only now can the truth be told."

Ben nodded, taking a final sip of his vodka and Mountain Dew, a drink the exact color of the water in the pool and motioned for another. "Drink, Chuck?" he asked.

"Dr. Pepper," Chuck said, patting a place on his bulging abdomen that could have been either his liver or his stomach. "I'm off the hard stuff."

I ordered another wine cooler.

"My landlady," Ben said, introducing me. "Carol, this is Chuck."

"Nice-looking landlady," Chuck said without really looking at me. "Never had any like her."

I smiled politely.

"Can you believe, Carol, that Chuck was in the service with me—on the same old tub?" Ben asked. "And now he's into this. Amazing."

"Hell, I've been into this for years. You should see my files," Chuck said, stroking his goatee. "But if I hadn't run into your ex and gotten your current address, you'd never have known about tonight—and, boy, would you have missed out!"

"Hey, I'm hip," Ben said and I winced. Ben had probably smoked dope all of two times and he'd practiced the language by the Berlitz method. I didn't have the heart to tell him that hip was over—dead. But hip or not, Ben was okay, the best roomer I'd had. Just before he arrived, I'd thrown out an old friend who never washed a dish in the half year she lived with me. She stuck me for two months rent and a $386.24 phone bill. Ben was a godsend. Navy and clean. With Ben, I was actually making house payments on time. Except for his radio—one talk show after another—he was fine.

Chuck popped open his Dr. Pepper. "Yes, sir, Ben, it was a great event! The aliens had a message, too. It's all documented. All of it. It's all in my newsletter. Hot last issue, huh, Ben, old boy? 'UFOs to Land in California!' How's that for a headline?"

"You betcha! Fantastic stuff! I mean, you got me where I live now. I'm going in for the heavy stuff now. After the Navy and my wife, I'm ready for the deep stuff. I know that the mind of man is just beginning—"

"Hey, Carol," Chuck interrupted, fixing me with his large colorless eyes. "Are you into the spiritual? Outer space? Other planes of existence? Astral travel? Is that why you're here?"

I started to say that I was here because Ben had paid me to drive him—his license having been suspended for driving while under the influence—but I caught Ben looking at me. "Well," I said to Chuck, "I don't rule any of it out. You know, I was even thinking of opening an astral travel agency. If it gets to be really popular, they'll be booking problems out there like everywhere else."

"UFOs are documented," Chuck said without batting an eye. "Our government has known about them for almost half a century. The alien leader told Ike they've been monitoring us since we tested the first A-bomb!"

"Amazing," said Ben.

"You've got it. Well, I'll go get dressed. Meet you two here in a bit. I've got to get Verna. She's a psychic. She thought she should come in case they don't want to talk. Telepathy's one of her things." He rushed off.

"Hey," said Ben, putting his hand over mine. I began to wonder if he'd already had too much to drink. "You're not sorry you came, are you? You heard what Chuck said. You could be on the spot for one of history's big events."

"We'll see," I said, pulling gently on my hand. "I want to make a phone call." I really wanted a break.

"Who are you calling? Some fellow?"

"My mother, Ben."

"Say hello to her for me."

"Okay, but she's got a boyfriend."

"Just hello."

Actually my mother has a boyfriend about as much as I do. Not much. I found phones between the lobby and the bar and stood in front of them. Suddenly, I did want to call someone. But who? Not my mother. If I told her what I was doing, she'd only say, "I'd rather sit home with egg on my face." My ex-husband? He's good to call about some things—like business. He's a CPA. I put him through school. I could call and say, "Hi there, Rick, I'm in the Hub-O-Tel in Barstow, Hub-of-the-Mojave, with the man who rents a room from me. No hanky-pank. We're waiting for a spaceship to land." No. A girlfriend once gave me the number of a man she phones. He's a foreigner and he'll accept collect calls from anywhere in the U.S. so he can practice his English. She says it's very soothing. You can talk to him about anything. I stared at the rows of buttons, then headed into the bar.

About a dozen men—from their clothes and conversations probably hunters, the kind who go into the desert and shoot small animals—were sitting around talking. I ordered a white wine and two of them turned up, one on each side. Bars are too easy. "Whoa!" I said when the wine came, "I'm a nun!" The one on my right laughed. I took the wine out to the pool.

When I got back to the table, Ben was sitting, head thrown back, eyes fastened like suction cups onto the sky. "See anything?" I asked.

"It's very moving," he said softly. "A night we'll always remember."

Chuck arrived wearing Bermuda shorts, a white shirt, and a bolo tie with a turquoise the size of a small child's fist. A tall, thin woman with a face like Trigger's and a tangle of graying blonde curls was with him.

"I read auras," said Verna, settling into the backseat of my Datsun and taking time to arrange yards of some bulky Third World fabric she was wearing. Ben got in back beside her, leaving Chuck to get into the front seat with me.

"That's great," I said. "You must have very good eyes."

"Turn left at the first light," Chuck said as I pulled out into the traffic. "After that, keep going."

"I'm getting nervous," Verna said.

"Picking up any vibes?" Chuck asked.

"Oh, I'm beginning to. There's this whirring sound."

"Hang in there, Verna," Chuck said, sounding like the coach at the rivalry game. "Now, Ben, as I was telling you back at the motel, the aliens warned Ike that we had to knock off with the atom bomb. Too risky. They'd already had to clean up our waste out in space."

"They sound like intelligent beings," Ben said.

"Highly intelligent. They told Ike that they could show us how to live without work, never run out of gas. The good life, but we weren't ready yet."

"Too much good news would be hard to take," I said.

"You're so right, sister," Chuck agreed.

"I think all this good news is giving me a headache," Ben said. "There's this throbbing here." In the rearview mirror I saw him touch his temple.

"Me too," Verna moaned. "Throbbing and humming . . . a buzzing sound. I'm sure it's them." Her head rolled back and she got ready to receive like a crystal set. Chuck meanwhile was scanning the skies, his forehead pressed against the windshield, his large head swiveling, a regular radar screen.

We drove on. And on.

"How did you learn about this projected arrival?" I asked Chuck. Ben had been vague about this.

"We have our ways, Carol, but since you're a friend of Ben's, I'll tell you. The aliens have sent some of their number amongst us. They look just like me and you. One of them phoned me just last week and told me to assemble people I could trust. Let me tell you it was hard getting that newsletter out in time! I've got over a thousand names on my mailing list!"

"Phoned you?" I asked.

"Turn here," Chuck said. I turned right through an open gate onto a narrow road.

"Phoned you?" A jackrabbit ran in front of my headlights, the only thing moving on the horizon.

"Yes. A man, an alien known to me only as Roy, called. We'd met before. He's one of them."

"They're coming," Verna muttered.

"Hot dog! What a night!" Chuck whooped.

At last we came to the edge of a vast paved area. "Used to be a World War Two landing strip," Chuck said. My lights picked up the gleam of chrome, lacquer, and aluminum as we passed perhaps forty or fifty cars, trailers, motor homes, and pickups, some towing boats, all facing east. "There's a line just like this on the other side," Chuck told us proudly. "When Roy gets the signal that they're going to land, we'll all turn on our headlights—sort of a welcome mat. That's Roy's motor home there.

He's saving a space for us. You'll like him, Ben. He's a good old boy. Pull right in there." I followed directions. "Yes sir," Chuck continued, "when these aliens get here, they're going to solve all of our problems. Hey, Verna, wake up! We're here. Yes, Ben, old buddy, from this night on, your ass is saved! Saved! Saved! Saved!" With that, Chuck bolted out of the car and began pumping Roy's hand.

Roy, for an alien, really had done a great job of disguising himself. He looked like a cousin of mine who worked in Seattle—the same lank hair, wiry body, even the same sort of J.C. Penney sport shirt and Hush Puppies. He was followed out of the motor home by a fat redhead wearing a Barry Manilow T-shirt and stretch pants.

Verna appeared to be snoozing, a slight snore coming from her flared nostrils. I let her be.

"Hey, Carol," Ben said, grabbing my arm a little unsteadily. Even in the dim light from the open door of Roy's motor home, I could see that his color was bad—sort of greasy gray.

"Carol," he said, trying to smile. "I guess I'm just overcome. Being here is too much. Great night... historic..." he gasped, stumbling toward Chuck.

"Sit down, Ben," I said.

"They're going to save us, Carol."

"Ben!"

He lurched forward, falling on his face. I knelt by him. He was breathing, but moaning with pain.

"Call an ambulance," I said to no one in particular.

"I'll get one on the CB," a man in the gathering crowd said.

"Can't have that," said Chuck, coming forward. "This meeting is supposed to be secret. Can't have ambulances, police all over the place."

"Secret! There're probably a couple of hundred people here!" I shouted, spinning up to face him.

"Oh, no," said the alien in a high raspy voice. "I just know they won't land if the police are here."

We compromised. Somebody radioed an ambulance to meet us at the gate. I drove there with Ben laboring for air and clutching his left arm, his eyes on the sky all the way. Finally, a light appeared on the horizon coming out of the south. "It's them," he said. "At last."

"I hope the hell it is," I said. Then we heard the siren.

I'd had five cups of machine-made coffee. All bad. I was starting on my sixth. The empty cups were lined up on the table in front of me. Out of the one window a strip of light like pale neon outlined the hills. Dawn.

Verna pushed open the door and came in. "I had Roy drop me off," she said breathlessly. "I'm good at healing, too. Can I see him? I can tell a lot by his aura."

"If he still has one," I said. "Ask the nurse. He had a heart attack. He's not doing well."

She slumped onto the seat beside me. "Got a safety pin?" she asked, pointing to a hole in her dress that gaped like a foolish mouth. "In the excitement I broke the zipper." I didn't think I had a pin, but I looked. No pin.

"So what happened after we left?" I asked.

"Oh . . . a lot. I was in a trance, of course. They communicated telepathically with me and with Roy. They decided not to land. I guess we here on earth still aren't ready." She sighed. I handed her my cup of coffee. She drank, making soft slurping sounds. "Chuck is trying to deal with his anger with you and Ben. He blames you for the bad vibes."

I shrugged. "Sneak past the nurse," I said when she'd finished the coffee. "He's in Intensive Care in the last bed. Squeeze his hand if he's awake. He'll be glad to see you."

"He seems like a nice man," she said. I nodded and watched her walk off down the hall, a tall, tired woman with a broken zipper. Then I counted the six paper cups and remembered a game I'd played with my brother. We each put a string through the bottom of a paper cup, knotted it, then pulled it tight across a room. I talked into the cup. He held it to his ear. Then we switched. We were supposed to hear each other. It never worked.

"I'm in the desert in a hospital. The man who rents a room from me—a nice man—may be dying. He came here to be saved by people from outer space, but they canceled," I said softly into the phone.

"Speak very slowly," said the voice at the other end. "My English is not yet good, but I want to understand what you are saying."

# Secrets

COOPER'S DOG was dying. It didn't seem to be in agony, but Cooper knew it was time to call the vet. Yet he couldn't bring himself to pick up the phone. If Cooper's father had been alive, the man would have gone outside, taken a shovel to the earth, dug a grave, brought the dog out, looked it in the eye, muttered something to it, and then put a bullet in its head. Southerners like his father knew about the bond between men and dogs. They knew that part of being a dog's master meant taking on life and death responsibilities.

But Cooper didn't even own a gun. No one he knew hunted. And he was embarrassed to ask his friends if they had a gun to offer him because he had the sort of friends who wouldn't admit to owning guns even if they did.

Cooper and his former wife had attended his father as he wasted away from lung cancer. They had waited with his father as the man's flesh moved closer to the bone—waited, watching him pull in cigarette smoke and then cough it out. Cooper's father smoked his last days away—smoked and looked out of the bedroom window at the winter field and the woods beyond, at the monochromatic grays of overcast sky and leafless tree scaffolds, oak on the high side, cypress on the low.

They tried to get his father to eat chicken gumbo with okra, his favorite dish, cooked by Roseanna, the black woman from down the road who came in once a week to clean a little and cook gumbos, and *étouffées,* and bisques, and fried greens with salt pork, meals only

Cooper and Janet ate until there was no more and Roseanna appeared again.

Smells from the old wood-frame Louisiana house also came back to Cooper—smells of the spices of the food and the resinous pine and oak burned in the fireplaces because the gas heat made his father gasp for air. And with those, the background smell of urine. The dog seemed to hate his own incontinence as much as Cooper's father had hated his. Tic-Tok left small puddles halfway to the newspaper, and these puddles, which Cooper cleaned and then wiped with white vinegar, sent pungent salty urine signals that Cooper associated with things being not as they should.

Cooper and Janet had let the dogs in every day for a visit to his father, the spotted bird dogs, twisting and panting around the legs of the bed, always damp, smelling of the fields, the woods, the distant outdoor places his father studied from the remove of his bed. And Tic-Tok, who had been a spoiled house dog in California, had to stay outside with his father's dogs in Louisiana, because dogs belonged outside, and when he came in with the other dogs for the daily visit he hated having to go outside again.

Tic-Tok was a mutt with maybe some Labrador, some Shepherd, some Dalmatian—not the sort of dog his father would have had. Although Cooper's father had liked Tic-Tok well enough, had taken burrs and ticks from the dog's coat after they'd walked across the hills of Marin when his father came to visit that one time.

Now Tic-Tok, the dog he and Janet had gotten from a box outside of a supermarket fifteen years ago when they'd both been students in Berkeley, was dying.

And as things would have it, yesterday he'd run into Janet. Right on Telegraph Avenue. As if seven years hadn't passed. She'd put on a little weight—not much—and she looked pretty, and he had a hard time at first remembering that he'd been married to her once, that she wasn't just an old friend whom he'd come across and was happy to see. She'd moved back to California a year ago and was living near Carmel and was in Berkeley visiting friends that day, people Cooper barely recalled and never saw. After a bit, she asked about the dog, almost as an afterthought, and he had to tell her that Tic-Tok was dragging himself around, not spending much time away from the pile of blankets, that his eyes were almost blinded by cataracts, that his kidneys were shot, and that it was just a matter of time.

"Oh, my God!" she'd said. "Oh, poor Tic-Tok." And then with the matter-of-factness he so often found disturbing in her but which had been comforting back when she changed his father's diapers, she said, "Pets outlive relationships, you know. They're usually a mistake. I left my dog with my parents when I went to school, and I left Tic-Tok with you. Just don't let him suffer."

"No," Cooper had said, suddenly shaky. "No. I won't." And then he said, "Well, would you like to see him before . . . ?"

"I don't know if I should, you know. For myself, I mean. I don't want to feel bad about things I'd almost forgotten."

"Well, he'll remember you. It might be nice to have a little whiff of you before he goes off to dog heaven."

She'd given him a strange look, as if he had taken leave of his senses, which then changed to a look that said that she should have remembered that Cooper was that sort of person. "Where do you live? I'll have some time tomorrow."

"I took him to the vet last week," Cooper said as soon as Janet entered. "He said Tic-Tok was going fast... and he offered to... you know, put him out of his misery. But I just couldn't ...." He stumbled and paused and felt that things should be clearly presented to Janet, but he didn't want to get into something emotional with her. He could feel her mind working as she looked around his cluttered, not-too-clean house, examining his paintings on the walls, the table where he had been doing watercolors— a medium he hadn't worked in when they'd been together.

"I'm teaching art in high school," he said. "It's a terribly poor neighborhood, down by the tracks in flatland, but a few of the kids really respond."

"Do you have time for your own work?"

"Not much. That's why I'm doing watercolors. Working wet on wet. I have to paint fast. They're a good thing for a person who doesn't have much time."

"They're nice," she said. She went over and looked. She touched the top painting, a misty Impressionistic landscape. She looked at the one under it, which was very much the same, a variation on the theme, and then didn't inspect more. He wasn't sure if she was incurious or being respectful of his privacy.

"He's in the bedroom."

"Do you live alone?"

"Yes," he said and then felt that she had gone too far, though it was a simple question. He began to wonder about having asked her here. She, as usual, had been skeptical of this visit right off, but he hadn't realized all the potential landmines until she stepped through the door. "He spends most of his time on an old electric blanket. I don't know if he's cold, but he shivers a lot."

"Oh, Tic-Tok," she said and went into the bedroom and knelt by the dog who did seem to recognize her, pounding his tail against the floor, lifting his head, whimpering, and trying to get to his feet, his paws sliding out from under him, his nails trying to claw some purchase on the wood. "Oh, poor Tic-Tok," she said, "poor old Tic-Tok."

"I don't think he's really in pain," Cooper said, kneeling beside Janet.

"No, but he's definitely failing. Why didn't you have the vet put him away? Why are you keeping him like this?"

"If my father were here, he'd shoot him."

Janet leaned back, sat on her heels, and appeared to think about this. "That's what he'd do," she said finally. "Well, you could do that."

"I don't have a gun," Cooper said. He stretched his hand out to the dog's tan shoulder. It made him uneasy talking like this in front of Tic-Tok. He wondered why he'd brought up the gun thing.

"I have a .thirty-eight in the car. It's a short-barreled revolver. Very easy to use. You can borrow it."

"You have a gun?" Cooper asked.

"My husband makes me carry it in the car," she said. "He was in Vietnam. While we were marching around here protesting, he was getting shot at. He believes in self-defense."

"Oh," Cooper said.

"He's very bright. He teaches at the language school

in Monterey. It's sort of a spy school. Do you know the
first thing they teach you to say in the language you're
learning?"

"Well, probably not 'peace.'"

"No." She laughed an abrupt laugh to signal she'd gotten the joke and studied Cooper with the same slide show
of expressions on her face as yesterday when he'd mentioned "dog heaven."

"They teach you to say, 'Don't shoot. I know secrets.'"

She left as briskly as she'd entered—circumspect,
avoiding any contact other than a handshake—and she
came back for a minute with the gun and placed it in its
leather holster on the kitchen counter next to half a can
of Alpo that he'd been diluting with broth. She usually
kept the gun in the glove compartment, she told him, but
she'd do without it. This was more important. She'd be
back up in a week for some workshop in investing and
she'd get it then. She was doing that now. Telling people
what to do with their money. He could picture her, brisk
and practical in one of those gray suits with a taupe blouse
that all the women seemed to wear who worked in the
financial district. MBA nuns, a friend had called them.

After Janet left, Cooper went back into the bedroom
and was surprised to realize that he longed for a cigarette,
though he'd quit smoking for good a month after his
father's death. Tic-Tok had managed to sit up, listing a
little to one side, but up. He slapped his tail on the floor
when Cooper came in and looked more alert than he had
for days. Maybe Janet's visit had done something for the
dog, or, maybe, and this thought distressed Cooper, the
dog was aware of the gun in the kitchen and was trying
to let Cooper know that he wasn't ready to go yet. He

was making an awful effort to look as if he was just resting between runs, that he could still fetch a stick or leap
for a Frisbee, a trick Cooper had delighted in teaching
him. All of these canine efforts at good cheer made
Cooper miserable.

Cooper remembered walking into his father's bedroom one time after a week of the man's steady decline to
find his father sitting up, a cigarette in one hand, another
burning in the ashtray. His father, usually calm, was
fidgeting and edgy. He got Cooper to help him stand and
walk to the window to look out at the view he saw every
day. Then he made Cooper support him for a walk
through the house, something he hadn't done for weeks.

In the living room, his father had turned around slowly
and then asked Cooper where he was. Cooper told him
that they were in the living room. It was the house they'd
moved into when Cooper was six. The place was old,
built in the last century in a then-popular style called
dogtrot because of the breezeway running through the
center onto which the rooms opened. When they moved
in, Cooper's father had the breezeway enclosed to create
a wide hall. The kitchen occupied a wing off the rear.
Sometime shortly after the move, Cooper's mother died
from a stroke, an unusual thing for such a young person,
and Roseanna started coming in to take care of Cooper
and his father.

Cooper's father had stood on the rag rug in the center
of the room and pivoted on his wobbling knees and said,
"Don't lie to me, boy. I'm in someone else's house."

"No sir," Cooper had said, puzzled because this was
the first time his father had ever been confused. "This is

your house. It's the house Uncle Wade left you. This is where I grew up."

"Don't lie to me, boy," his father said, angry and shaking as he hung onto Cooper's arm. "I know where I am and where I'm not." Then tears started to run from his father's eyes, large tears that fell onto the floor. His father didn't sob or make any crying sounds. He just let these large tears fall as Cooper turned him back to the hall and walked him to the bedroom. Once in bed with the familiar view again, the man seemed to relax a little. He stopped crying. As he leaned onto the pillows and Cooper brought up the covers, his father said, "You know, there's a lot I've never told you."

"Yes sir," Cooper said, "I expect there is."

His father then lit another cigarette and studied the world beyond the window. He didn't get up to walk around again and he didn't question where he was. In fact, he hardly spoke. In three days he was dead.

Often, since that afternoon, Cooper had wondered why he hadn't asked his father what it was his father hadn't told him. He wondered why he had shied away from asking his father some question that would have prolonged that conversation. What had he been reluctant to hear then, that afternoon, with the smell of cigarette smoke and wood smoke in the air? What could his father have wanted to say?

His father could, perhaps, have told his son of another life he'd led, a life he'd never revealed. There were stories of such death-bed confessions. Cooper has tried to imagine his father leaning forward, regaining his color through the vivid palette of memory as he whispered of infidelities into his son's ear.

Cooper has also considered that his father might have

wanted to recount ways in which Cooper had managed to fall short of certain standards and failed to meet expectations. There had been an incident one autumn when Cooper was fourteen and he'd gone with two cousins on his first coon hunt. Cooper loved the dogs, the lanky black-and-tans, and he'd been almost feverish with excitement as they drove up into Mississippi. They arrived after dark at a clearing in a woods to find other pickup trucks already there and waiting, the men with their guns passing in and out of the beams of light, the dogs still on the trucks, quivering in their cages.

Cooper followed the men who followed the dogs, the high clear hound voices—all of them thrashing between trees, getting soaked up to their knees in creeks. Whenever they'd paused, the headlamps they wore drilled minerlike tunnels into the blackness and there was always someone to hand him a flask.

He was reeling with whiskey and fatigue when the dogs finally treed a raccoon. While their lights fastened the animal, huge with anger—its eyes already distant with foreknowledge—the men argued whether to kill it on the branch or shoot it down for the dogs to fight. Finally, one of his cousins won the chance to bring it down.

Everyone agreed the shot was perfect as the live raccoon tumbled to the dogs. In the shadows, Cooper vomited. All of the way home, in the heated air of the cab, he kept smelling the rubbed-away vomit on his clothes. "My nose tells me that old Cooper lost it back there," his younger cousin said.

"Shut up," the older cousin, the one who'd made the much-praised shot, answered. "You'll do better next time, Coop." There had never been a next time. Cooper had always been sure that someone must have told his father about this and yet his father never mentioned it, though Cooper waited for him to bring it up.

Then, too, it was also possible that his father might have decided to share some new and fearful insight, some apprehension, with Cooper. He might have wanted to say that he'd had a glimpse into the abyss and seen nothing but darkness, no remedy of light.

But as he stood beside his father staring down into the weave of the blanket, Cooper had no list of pending truths or revelations. He just felt a need not to hear what his father had to say.

Cooper ran his hand from Tic-Tok's head along his back to his tail and scratched the spot just at the base of the spine. The dog relaxed, lay down, and then closed his eyes. Cooper continued scratching and was pleased to see that Tic-Tok was enjoying this enough to slap his tail once on the floor.

When the dog was asleep, Cooper went to the kitchen to put on water for coffee. He was starting a new unit tomorrow with his beginning class. It was going to be a sculpture project and the students were supposed to bring things from their homes that were going to be thrown away. He planned to gather his own collection of refuse for a demonstration and for the kids who invariably forgot the assignment and arrived empty handed.

As soon as he entered the kitchen, there was the gun. He had never had a gun in his house before, and its solid metal presence on the white-and-yellow speckled Formica counter, beside the Alpo, in front of the glass canisters filled with sugar, flour, and coffee—just one more domestic object—gave Cooper a sense of vertigo.

He did not normally drink by himself, but he had a bottle of Jack Daniels in a cabinet. He reached over the gun, opened the cabinet, and took out the bottle and a glass, poured several ounces, and sat on a stool to consider things. His father had always stated his belief in the advisability of spending some quiet time with a glass of whiskey before taking any actions that might recast the universe in unpredictable ways.

The hillside behind Cooper's house rose sharply, its broken face covered with wide-leafed English ivy. He had neighbors above, below, and on either side—all people who he knew held sacrosanct the virtue of quiet. The sound of the gun would not pass unnoticed. With the whiskey making a warm spot beneath his lungs, he held the gun in his hand and felt its weight. It was a solid thing, an admirable example of form following function. He didn't allow himself to think about Janet holding it.

He had always been good at hitting targets—darts, archery, shooting—when he was younger. But that had been years ago. He took a beer bottle out of the trash and brought it to the edge of the property and placed it on a stump against the backdrop of ivy. Then he walked back, turned, took aim. The light was fading but the glint of glass in the setting sun was enough.

The sound was deafening and the kick unexpected. His arm flew up as if it belonged to a puppet. It took him a moment to recover. Then he went over to the stump. The bottle had disappeared. He saw a bit of the paper label off to the right.

Back in the house he expected the phone to be ringing. He listened for the sound of a siren. He looked out of the window in the front to see a flashing red light. Nothing.

There was no evidence that anyone had heard the shot.

Except in the bedroom. Tic-Tok had managed to crawl under the bed, leaving only a few inches of tail showing beyond the spread. "Oh, Jesus, I'm sorry, boy," Cooper said and threw himself on the bed above the dog. He lay very still knowing the dog knew he was there, hoping to suck in, absorb like a sponge, the animal's fears.

A few moments later, Cooper noticed he still had the gun in his hand. He released it gently onto the night table and went to sleep. Sometime later he woke up with the knowledge that things were worse. He turned on the light and saw Tic-Tok, on his side, legs up, the right hind paw scratching at something invisible. It seemed an involuntary action, something done without Tic-Tok's approval, a spasm. Cooper rolled onto the floor and crawled next to the dog. "Tic-Tok, old boy," he whispered into the dog's ear. The dog's eyes were open, but staring, unfocused. The dog's breathing was rusty, an act done against itself. "Ohhh, Tic-Tok... Tic-Tok ...." he said. "I'm here, boy. I'm here."

He lay next to the dog for an hour. Nothing improved. The breathing sounded even more difficult. Cooper got up and sat on the bed and called the vet and got the answering service. He asked for the vet he usually saw and was told that he was out of town but that he was having his calls taken by someone else who, yes, would make a house visit.

Cooper poured another glass of whiskey and sat beside Tic-Tok. Neither he nor Janet had been in the room when his father had died. At first, Cooper felt terribly guilty that he hadn't been there holding his father's hand, but later it occurred to him that, perhaps, his father, always a private man, had wanted to do it alone.

The doorbell rang.

When Cooper opened the door he couldn't figure out why a young woman was ringing his bell at 11:30 at night. Then he understood that she was the vet, and the leather pouch over her shoulder was her doctor's bag.

"He's in the bedroom," Cooper said and stood aside to let her pass.

She knelt beside the dog and Cooper knelt beside her. Her hair was wet and Cooper realized it was raining outside. That seemed like a good thing, but he couldn't think why. She was quiet and attentive to Tic-Tok, in a way Cooper liked.

"We should do it, you know," she said. She had a simple authority in her voice. Cooper nodded.

"He isn't going to get any better."

Cooper nodded again.

"Should I?"

He nodded.

"Do you want to be here with him?"

"Yes," Cooper said, and didn't recognize his own voice, it seemed to have come from so far away.

"It's called Permasleep," she said. "It's very quick and painless."

"Good-bye, Tic-Tok," Cooper said and put his hand on the ruff of fur that crept up under the collar. He squeezed the loose skin and held on.

His father had been lucid until the end. Both he and Janet had learned to give shots of Demerol, then morphine. The doctor had stopped in twice a day. They had all worked to honor his father's wish to die at home, to be able to spend his last days looking at his field, at the woods beyond, under the tin roof of his own house.

Cooper knew he had tried to do what his father had requested, but what still bothered him was what he had not allowed his father to say.

As he sat on the floor beside the twitching dog, the realization struck Cooper that his father had had no message to deliver that afternoon—that his father had no special intelligence to impart to his son, but had merely wanted to buy some time with talk, to extend his days among the living through the simple act of speech. It struck Cooper that he had failed to understand that his father might have wanted to say nothing more significant than to express an opinion on the right diet for dogs, or the stupidest thing to do in a duck blind, or to ramble on about something he'd never liked—collards, for instance —that he'd never have to eat again.

Cooper felt Tic-Tok slump forward. The dog was collapsing, but gently, easily, almost in slow motion.

"You made the right decision, you know," she said. "You might have missed." She was standing now watching him.

"Thank you," Cooper said. It didn't make any sense but he felt she wanted to reassure him and he could let her. Then he realized that she had seen the gun on the nightstand.

"I'll let myself out," she said.

Cooper nodded. The dog's head was already heavy on his lap, pressing him down, pinning him to the ground, making him weightless.

# Bougainvillea

MYRTA PUT THREE cubes in the glass, poured in the orange juice, and then the vodka—a light touch on the vodka. This was, after all, breakfast. Then because the air conditioner wasn't working, she went to stand by the open door.

The other trailers in the park were already shimmering like silver sausages on a griddle, and it looked to Myrta as if there were a half-hearted mirage between her and space seventeen across the driveway. Not even the bougainvillea held up on a day like today.

She barely had time for a sip or two when she saw Frank heading her way. She couldn't believe it. She thought she'd seen the last of him some years ago. But then, after a moment's reflection, she realized that she wasn't surprised at all. She knew his sign. He was a Cancer. He held on. But she was upset anyway.

Frank was trouble. She didn't need his kind of trouble either—hanging around her, wanting to fix her washer, buy her a blender, a new color television. Besides, now Will was hanging around and he was a lot easier to deal with. She pulled back from the door and sat down.

Except here was Frank, "Big as life and twice as ugly," as he would have said. Frank. And yet...

"Hiya, kid!" he said into the open door.

"Well, shoot!" she said, pulling herself out of her chair and pulling the muumuu out and around her in a graceful way. She then reached up and fluffed her hair and was glad she'd bothered to henna it just last week, even though henna was a big nuisance. "It's Frank, isn't it?"

He was already inside the screen door, though he'd had the sense to leave his suitcase outside. He knew how she'd squawk if he brought it inside the trailer.

He grabbed her and squeezed her hard, pulling her next to him, her bulk a cushion for his sharpness. His kiss was hard on her lips and his tongue was fighting its way between her teeth. And then she was his—just like always.

Later, when they were both naked on the bed, sweltering with the curtains closed because of the neighbors, he said, "You're the best, Myrta. I don't know why. I mean there are lots of women in this world and I've had my share. I'm not a young man, and, by and large, I've had my share, but you're the best."

And Myrta shifted slightly and closed her eyes and just wanted to rest. She dozed a little. When she woke, she knew she'd snored because her throat was rough.

Frank was in his shorts. He'd found the vodka and orange juice and he was just sitting there on her bed drinking and watching her.

She turned over to look at him. "You got new teeth," she said. She hadn't noticed before.

"The better to eat you with, Granny," he said, putting the vodka down and reaching over to slide his hands under her breasts, which these days hung down almost to her belly.

So it began again.

And she forgot to tell Frank about Will.

Then someone knocked at the door of the trailer. She knew it was Will.

"Get dressed," she whispered hoarsely to Frank, who was asleep.

Will was already inside with the refrigerator door open. He had his own bottle of vodka and he was stuffing it into the freezer where nothing was really frozen.

She had the muumuu on by then.

Will saw her and reached his arm around her and nuzzled his lips into the folds of her neck. She reached around him. He was ample—almost as wide as she was. She liked the feel of Will. He was substantial, and yet . . .

Frank was in the bedroom.

"Hi, honey," Will finally said, when she'd let him go. "I had a hell of a day. Everybody in town went fishing today, it's so darn hot. Sold tackle and lots of bait. I'm bushed." And he collapsed on the built-in sofa.

She mixed Will a vodka and 7-Up and handed it to him. He drank it gratefully in three gulps. She counted. Then she made another and sat down on the place he patted on the sofa beside him. He started hugging and nuzzling again.

That was when Frank came in.

"What the hell you think you're doing, Myrta?" Frank asked.

"Oh, for Pete's sake, Frank," she said suddenly tired. "What do you mean?"

Will was on his feet, but not really ready for anything. He would as soon as offered his hand as not, Myrta knew.

"This here is Will Duggan, Frank," she said out of the great tiredness. "And I gave him the block out of the Chevrolet."

"Looks like you gave him more than the block," Frank said.

Will sat down again as though accounted for. Myrta felt now that she was underwater, swimming somewhere out where she didn't want to be. She'd never cared for swimming anyway. She'd always been too plump to move through the water quickly like the other girls.

"And besides," Frank said, squaring off, "that's my Chevrolet and you can't give away my block."

"That Chevrolet was totaled," Myrta said, pulling herself to the surface and looking around, "and I didn't think you were ever coming back."

"Well, I never knew that was your block," Will said, on his feet again.

"Come outside and say that," Frank said.

Will shifted his weight back and forth.

Myrta had surfaced now. She was floating, something she was good at, and she was watching them both.

"I knew you looked funny when you came out of that bedroom," Will said to her and took a stance opposite Frank.

"Why don't you two go outside," she said.

"Outside," Will echoed and opened the door and went out. Frank, his eyes on Will, followed.

Myrta turned away and went to the sink and looked down at the glasses there. She heard them out in the dusk. There were blows that connected, and some that didn't. There were sighs and hard breathing. When she finally looked out of the window, they were out there where the mirage had been, hugging each other and rolling over and over, lean and thick, over and over in an embrace that, had she been able to envy anything at all, she would have envied.

She watched them from the steps of the trailer. Her red muumuu flared around her like a dark torch. She heard only the sobs.

In the end, she went back inside and put her hands over

her ears so as not to hear the sobs, which by now were not loud.

Then she placed her hand on her phone. Suddenly she wanted to phone "After Dark Dave," who had the call-in radio show, and talk to him—talk to everybody with their radios on—let them hear her voice stretched and thin, floating away down the highway ahead of their headlights as they drove. She wanted to say, "I never did understand. I never did understand it." But she didn't call.

The sobbing stopped and she turned and went back to the open door. She saw Will's back under the streetlight at the end of the row of trailers. He was going away.

Frank was standing in the shadow of the bougainvillea bush. The blossoms were a bright scarlet with the light behind them.

"Get a flashlight, Myrta," he said.

"What?"

"I lost my teeth. Help me look for them."

She got the light and together they searched until she found them lying in a deep shadow. The light from her flashlight showed them like two tiny pink sea creatures lightly coated with dust.

# Burning Joan

J OAN OF ARC stood in her cart on the way to her pyre, her eyes on the jeering crowd. They'd taken away her armor. They made her wear a gown. They weren't going to let her save them after all. It never occurred to either Isabel or me as we stared at the bright screen in the dark auditorium of Holy Redeemer School that Joan was anything but the kind of person we would want to be. We'd each donated a can of food for a benefit movie for the poor of our parish. I brought beets and Isabel brought spinach, and we were getting every ounce's worth of beauty, bravery, and martyrdom.

"I wonder what I'd look like if I cut my hair," Isabel said as we blinked in the afternoon sun, startled not to be in France after all, but in Marigny, Louisiana, beside the rectory parking lot.

"No, not your hair," I said. My hair was dark and curly and my mother insisted that I keep it short. Isabel's hair was long ropy blonde, the kind of hair only one person in a thousand gets. Isabel didn't look much like Joan. She had a tipped-up nose and an overbite, but the fact that she would even consider cutting her hair seemed like a step on a road somewhere. Everyone knew that cutting hair was the first stage to renunciation of the world. Nuns cut their hair.

"You could do it while my mother's at work."

"Think about it a little first," I said. Isabel's mother had beautiful hair, too. I didn't think she'd understand if I cut her daughter's. She wasn't the saintly type.

"I'm still thinking," she said the next day as we stretched out on the sandy strip of beach by the lake. There Phillip Duvall sat, with the kind of egalitarianism we admired him for, not on the high chair for lifeguards but with his back against one of the supports of the chair. He was surrounded by everyone important in our world. There was talk that he'd get a football scholarship to LSU. He'd just broken up with someone, and now four senior girls lay on towels beside him. They were all shapely and beautiful and wise and wonderful enough to be kind to me and Isabel. I was eleven and Isabel almost twelve. They considered us pets.

It was flattering to have them know our names, but when I sat beside them I felt hopeless and unformed, like a lump of dough. The problem was, however, that I wasn't lumpy and neither was Isabel. We were tube shaped, completely without bumps or curves or mysterious shaded regions.

"Isabel's thinking of cutting her hair," I told them.

"Oh, no," one of them said. She had black hair that curled under at the ends and perfect teeth. The others echoed her.

"I won't marry you if you cut your hair," Phillip Duvall said.

"Do you believe he's actually thought of marrying me?" Isabel asked. We were sitting in her bedroom with the fan on playing gin rummy.

"He said it."

"But he was joking, wasn't he?"

"He wouldn't have said it if it hadn't crossed his mind."

"He's the most beautiful man in the world," she said. "I could be Mrs. Phillip Duvall—after he gets out of LSU."

"He's seven years older than you are."

"He'll wait if he loves me."

"Suppose he wants to kiss you. Will you let him?"

"Oh, Holy Mary," she said and put down the cards. "I don't know how to kiss. I don't want him to kiss me until I know how. We have to practice, Kate." She leaned over the cards, her mouth puckered, her eyes on me.

"Girls don't kiss girls."

"How do we learn then? Think about it."

"It's weird—girls kissing."

"What's weirder, kissing a girl, or not knowing how to kiss at all?"

As usual, Isabel made her point. I shrugged and closed my eyes, but I wasn't prepared for the aggressiveness of her mouth, for the muscular properties of lips. "Kiss back," she said, taking a breath. I didn't know whether to tighten or loosen. "You're terrible." We tried again, I relaxed this time and let her mouth take over, letting my lips do what hers did. We fell over backwards onto the pillows. "It's okay," she said. "We're girls."

That same afternoon we burned Bo Peep. In second grade, when we'd become friends, I'd been impressed by Isabel's collection of Storybook Dolls. She had a row of them lined up on a bookshelf with their full-skirted stiff dresses, wide-open eyes, and swirls of hair. Her aunt sent them to her. Isabel wasn't particularly interested in dolls, but she knew these were enviable. Their arms were jointed, but not their legs. They weren't made to be played with.

We stripped Bo Peep of her finery and dressed her in a tunic we made from an old sheet. When we'd bound the dress with a piece of dark twine, it was not unlike what

Joan had worn. We borrowed a small red wagon from the driveway of the house next door and put Joan into it and jounced her behind the shed where we assembled a pyre from fallen pine branches. We placed a fairly straight branch in the center for a stake and tied the doll to it.

The dried pine needles caught fire immediately. Flames lost no time licking Joan's feet and igniting her dress. The doll, celluloid, flared briefly, then caved in on itself, the small glass eyes bulging before they dripped away from the head. The hair smoldered at first, then shot into sparks and soon also disappeared into ashes. The whole event probably lasted no more than five minutes. We sat back on our heels amazed at what we had done.

"What's that smell?" Isabel's grandmother called from the back door. She was supposed to watch us, but she almost never left her room where she sat each day reading novels.

"We're getting ready to roast marshmallows," Isabel answered, rolling her eyes at me.

"Don't set anything on fire!" The screen door slammed shut.

"Let's go to the store and get marshmallows," said Isabel.

"And Coke," I said. My throat was dry. I felt as if I had a fever.

We had the world to ourselves that summer. My own family faded into a benign pallor as Isabel's mostly absent family became mine. Her mother, who looked like an older, more assured version of Isabel, was divorced—a distinction of some kind in those days. She worked as a legal secretary for the district attorney and rarely appeared when I was there. Isabel's brother, Nick, who was rumored to be the smartest boy in school, was gone for most of the summer visiting cousins in New Orleans. When Isabel's grandmother made a foray from her room, it was usually only to leave money on the table for Isabel to do the family shopping. She always left enough for us to buy Cokes and candy and a magazine—usually a *True Confessions* or a *Photoplay.*

Each afternoon Isabel and I rode our bikes to the beach, and, after swimming, rode back to her house waving away the yellow jackets that followed our wet hair. We played cards, talked, and kissed occasionally. We were practicing for boys. We also burned Little Miss Muffet, Sleeping Beauty, Little Red Riding Hood, the Queen of Hearts, and Snow White.

On the day Nick got back, his friend Charlie came over. Nick had changed. He'd put on a little weight, maybe even muscle. He'd been quiet before, interested only in the chemistry lab he'd set up in his bedroom, try-ing to frighten us with stories about how he was about to make nitroglycerine and blow us up. Now he swaggered and wanted to talk. As he and Charlie and Isabel and I sat in the kitchen eating tuna sandwiches, I watched Nick chew and wondered whether he was good-looking or not. He and Charlie were going to be sophomores at St. Ignatius High in the fall.

"I went on Bourbon Street with my cousins," he told Charlie as we listened. "They're at Tulane. They knew a guy at the door and they got me in to see a stripper. Her name was Tempest and she took off all her clothes but two little stars on her nipples and a tiny G-string. They said that sometimes she takes off everything and sits on guys' laps."

"What do you do to get to see her take off everything?" Charlie asked, pulling off his glasses and rubbing the lenses with the bottom of his T-shirt. His fingers were long and moved constantly like insect antennae.

"What were the stars on her nipples made of?" asked Isabel.

"How the hell do I know?" said Nick. "They were shiny. She had big tits and her skin was really white. She probably sleeps all day."

"Like a bat," I said.

Charlie laughed and Nick scowled at him.

"I'd like to see a stripper," said Isabel.

Later that afternoon Nick pushed open Isabel's door while we were lying together on the bed.

"Don't you know about knocking?" said Isabel.

"I have this present from Aunt Inez that I'm supposed to give you. Besides, you're my sister."

"Probably another dumb doll." Isabel took the gift-wrapped box from him. "Thanks."

"Drop dead," he said and slammed the door.

"Cinderella," she said after tearing off the paper. "Wouldn't you know?"

"Poor Cinderella." I started to laugh and then Isabel laughed too. We rolled around on the floor and held our stomachs when they began to hurt.

They had been smoking cigarettes that night and they had a bottle of rum. Isabel's mother was at a meeting. "We're making Cuba Libres," said Nick. He and Charlie stood in front of the refrigerator putting ice in a couple of glasses. "That's what everyone at Tulane drinks."

"Make me and Kate one," said Isabel.

"No way," said Nick.

"Aw, don't be so hard on them," said Charlie.

"They're just kids." Nick handed Charlie a glass.

"Just one drink," Isabel said.

"Why not?" said Charlie. "Let them have fun, too."

Nick frowned and looked from me to Isabel and then back to me. "Do you really want a drink?"

"Sure," I said. Isabel nodded.

"Okay," Nick said, "But you have to drink in my room and promise not to tell."

"We're not going to tell," said Isabel.

The drinks weren't bad. They were mostly Coke with rum and a little bit of lemon juice. Nick had twin beds in his room. He sat on one and Charlie on the other. Isabel and I sat on the floor beneath a table loaded with glass tubes and vials. Nick and Charlie kept leaning over and whispering while we drank. We finished the first, and Nick made us each a second. When we were about halfway done with those, Nick leaned back on his pillow. "Charlie thinks you two ought to do a striptease for us. Charlie thinks you two are cute."

"Hey wait!" said Charlie, spitting out some of his drink. "You were the one talking about getting girls to strip."

"Yeah, okay," said Nick. "Who cares whose idea it is?" He turned to us. "It's not just taking off your clothes. It's dancing, too."

"What do we wear?" asked Isabel.

"I don't know," said Nick. "Get something out of Mother's room. Use your imagination."

"How much do we have to take off?" I asked. I was a little uneasy about how quickly Isabel seemed willing to go along, but the idea was intriguing. It seemed to belong with drinking, to be a buoyant and spinning thing to do.

"As much as you want," said Nick.

My mother had utility white underwear. Isabel's mother had lace and colors, but everything was too big for me. When I put on a black bra, the cups crumpled over my chest.

"Stuff it with something," Isabel said.

"No. Then when I take it off the stuffing will fall out. That'll look dumb."

"Are you really going to do this, Kate?" Her question surprised me. I thought she'd been all for it.

"Sure," I said. Now that I was getting dressed, I wanted to—but not by myself. I took another swallow of the drink and noticed that Isabel's was almost finished.

"Her drawers are going to be too big for you."

I had on a pair of black panties trimmed with lace. When I let go, they slid down over my hips. My own were cotton with tiny flowers. "I'll use a ribbon and scrunch mine up on the sides to make them littler." I wanted to ask her how far she would go, but I was feeling bolder than I'd ever felt, adventurous, and I didn't want to give her an excuse to back out.

Isabel had on pink panties and a pink bra. She pulled out a black slip and handed it to me. "You look good in black. Black's sexy." The slip was silky. It came almost to my ankles. I looked in the mirror and took a lipstick from the dresser and put it on. I smeared some on my cheeks. I drew darker eyebrows. I lined my eyes. I gave my chin a beauty mark. I didn't look like myself at all.

Nick and Charlie had been busy, too. Nick had brought in the phonograph from the living room. They'd turned off the lights except for two gooseneck lamps that shot beams onto a cleared patch of floor.

As soon as Isabel and I got into the room, I felt different. Charlie and Nick sat behind the lights, their faces in shadow. Nick put on a record—Louis Armstrong. "They always strip to trumpets," he said.

"Let's do it together," I said. Isabel looked relieved.

Neither of the boys objected to our not going singly. They were probably as surprised by all of this as we were.

When the music began, both Isabel and I giggled. Instead of feeling sexy, I felt dazed. I couldn't remember why I was standing there, but it seemed as if we'd made a pact and had to go through with it. Isabel put her hands up in the air and wiggled her bottom and turned around. I recognized it as part of the hokey-pokey and did it, too. It seemed like a good way to begin. We did a little bit of hula too, although the rhythm wasn't right.

"Take it off," said Nick. Charlie joined in and they both chanted.

I don't know who went first, but as soon as I'd tossed the slip to the floor, I looked over at Isabel and she was in bra and panties, too. I decided not to watch her anymore. I closed my eyes and listened only to the trumpet. I slid the bra off my shoulders and let it fall down around my hips. I felt like a snake wriggling out of its skin. I sneaked a look through half-shut eyes and saw that the lights had turned my body white. I stared down at my nipples, flat and hard as coins, my feet moving on the scarred wood floor, as distant as stars. I reached for my panties and pulled them down. It was awkward, but I knew it had to be done.

When the overhead light went on, I opened my eyes and saw that we were both naked, stepping up and down on two small islands of abandoned underwear. Isabel's mother stood in the doorway.

She gave us time to get dressed, then came into Isabel's room and sat beside us on the bed. I could tell that she'd been drinking, too. Her breath was sour. Her beautiful hair was messy and her lipstick was almost gone except for a thin outline. She looked at Isabel first, then me, then sighed and fixed her eyes on a spot across the room.

"God wants you to stay pure," she said. "Girls should be pure." She looked tired and I could tell right away that she had no heart for this, but that she believed she had to do it. "Boys don't understand that you're really pure inside. If you do things like you did tonight, they'll take advantage of your innocence. You should learn to pray for the strength to resist."

Neither Isabel nor I looked at each other while she spoke. I turned my eyes down to the bedspread. It was white chenille. I plucked at the tufts and rolled the threads that came out into little balls.

She left us alone and went to her own bedroom. I was supposed to spend the night with Isabel, but as we undressed—for the second time that evening—I felt a pain, like a buzz saw sounds, right behind my forehead. "I have to go home," I said. "I have a headache."

"You probably need glasses," said Isabel. She sat in her pink shortie pj's examining her face in a hand mirror. She hadn't managed to get off all the mascara and her eyes had a smudgy, old-movie star look.

"I'm going home," I said and began pulling on my T-shirt.

"Just take two aspirin." She'd put down the mirror and was glaring at me. It wasn't hard to tell that she was annoyed.

I broke the cardinal rule of constant contact the next morning by not calling Isabel as soon as I'd eaten breakfast, but I was ready when her call came. "Come on over after lunch," she said. "We're not finished."

Isabel's mother was at work as usual and Nick was off, probably shooting baskets. In the drowsy summer stillness, we dressed Cinderella as Joan, then rattled her along the driveway in her cart and tied her to a stake made from a piece of broken lattice. We were driven by a sense of urgency, a need for haste. We built a pyre higher than any before and stood back while the first young flames sprang up. I looked over them to Isabel and our eyes met. Neither of us could control our smiles and I knew that her heart was pounding, too. The fire raced up to the larger twigs. We backed away as the doll's tunic turned first brown then black and the tiny figure became a torch that burst open to reveal flames licking inside. The blond hair ignited into a joyously bright crown as sparks shot into the air and sappy twigs burst like firecrackers.

"We loved Joan," I said when it was over and we stood staring down at the charred circle in the grass. "Why did we want to burn her?"

"She asked for it," said Isabel.

My glee was gone. I felt old, older even than the girls on the beach. As I pedaled home into the breezeless afternoon,

I wanted only to outdistance the smell of smoke that clung to my hair and clothes.

A little later, lying in the tub with a tower of lather on my head, I decided that no matter what my mother said, I'd let my hair grow and grow. I closed my eyes and, for a moment, I could already feel it brushing my shoulders.